Love's Beautiful Dream

JUNE MASTERS BACHER

HARVEST HOUSE PUBLISHERS
Eugene, Oregon 97402

Scripture quotations are taken from the King James Version of the Bible.

Dedicated to
all those who said,
"One day you will!"

LOVE'S BEAUTIFUL DREAM

Copyright © 1987 by Harvest House Publishers
Eugene, Oregon 97402

ISBN 0-89081-577-1

Printed in the United States of America.

OTHER MEMORABLE BOOKS
by June Masters Bacher

❀

The Love Is a Gentle Stranger Series

An adventurous saga of the American frontier and a young woman's quest to find a new beginning.

Book 1 *Love Is a Gentle Stranger*
Book 2 *Love's Silent Song*
Book 3 *Diary of a Loving Heart*
Book 4 *Love Leads Home*

The Journey To Love Series

The continuing story of Rachel Buchanan and Colby Lord along the Frontier Trail to Oregon.

Book 1 *Journey To Love*
Book 2 *Dreams Beyond Tomorrow*
Book 3 *Seasons of Love*
Book 4 *My Heart's Desire*

The Love's Soft Whisper Series

Book 1 *Love's Soft Whisper*
Book 2 *Love's Beautiful Dream*

Quiet Moments—A Daily Devotional for Women

❀

Contents

For we walk by faith,
not by sight.
2 Corinthians 5:7

Chapter 1

The Magical Month

June! The magical month was approaching rapidly.

Wrapped in her robe, raven hair tossed carelessly over slender shoulders, Courtney sat at her desk in the dim light of the late-May dawn. The birds had awakened her early of late. She welcomed their twitter, as there was so much to do in preparation for her end-of-June wedding—letters to compose, lists to make, and daily the all-important entry to make in her pre-nuptial journal. Her private, sacred thoughts. Her hopes. Her dreams. And, above all, her all-consuming love and commitment to the wonderful man whom God had brought her to the Western frontier to meet . . . those beautiful words that one is never able to voice above the pounding of the heart when one is in love. Written down, those thoughts would be her wedding gift to Clint.

Spring had come back to the Columbia Valley, melting the last of the snow into triumphant streams that rushed to the mighty river—taking with them the remnants of Courtney's bitter memories. With a sort of childish grace, the girl, who seemed to look familiar to so many because of her striking resemblance to a Renaissance painting of a sad-sweet-faced Madonna, rose from the slipper chair and hurried to the window.

"Oh, what a magnificent morning, Lord!" she whispered softly as she threw open the sash to let in a burst of dew-fresh air. Even from here, her nostrils could catch the faint odor of Donolar's roses on his Isle of Innisfree.

"It is good to be alive. It is good that my brother's roses will yet be in bloom when I become the wife of the man You gave me," Courtney whispered in prayer. Those words she would enter in the journal, which was more a collection of prayers than her busy-day activities. In fact, each one began with "Dear God."

Breathing in the rose-scented breeze, Courtney wondered what her life would have been like if her mother, for reasons of her own, had not bundled her away to be with Cousin Arabella. Would she be marrying Lance, her childhood sweetheart? Would Mother have approved of that? She approved of nothing else about her dark-haired daughter, a "throwback to the mining Glamoras" and not at all like her own royal line (as were the rest of the children). Vanessa, the only sister, Efraim, the oldest of the family . . . and Efraim's fraternal twin, whom Courtney had found here, with no knowledge of his identity. They were all fair-haired—acceptable in Mother's sight—except for Donolar who, though Bellevue-fair, was "different." So he was exiled, too.

Of one thing Courtney was certain: She would not have come to meet God face-to-face in the shallow Eastern circles that Mother and Vanessa thought of as absolutes. Neither would she have come to appreciate Cousin Bella . . . discover dear Donolar . . . nor Clint Desmond. Oh, the wonder of it all!

"It was like throwing Brer Rabbit in the briar patch, wasn't it, Lord?" Courtney whispered without a touch of irreverence.

The sun had climbed the other side of the mountain range, bringing a wash of amber to the lushness of the ever-enlarging maple leaves and gilding the tips of each needle on the coniferous forest that lay untouched around the Mansion-in-the-Wild. Courtney felt the familiar lift of spirit as she craned her neck to see the strange angles and ells of the great house—a mixture of architecture that said neither fire, flood, nor time could destroy it.

"This place, so beloved by Cousin Bella, Clint, Donolar, and all others who enter its gates—those possessed with a heart, anyway—is like love, isn't it, Lord?"

The idea was not new. Each renovation seemed to spell out a growing love, making the whole of it a union of something greater than the sum of the old Mansion's parts. This was the secret that she and Clint had discovered, the secret that maybe nobody else on earth knew, Courtney thought with growing wisdom beyond her 18 years. The ring on her engagement finger was proof, she thought as she touched the great pearl, which had belonged to his great-grandmother and grandmother before him. His mother, sad to say (like her own mother), put more value on earthly things than on treasures in heaven. How could they have been so blind, making no effort to create a happy, lasting union . . . making a mate feel loved, appreciated, and desired . . . and knowing she was loved in return? It took no grand gestures; the little things counted more.

Courtney frowned. Weddings were for families. Both Clint and she should have their mothers here. But who knew where either was to be found? Clint had said a little bitterly that he did not so much as know his mother's name. After all, she had made meaningless trips to the altar three times . . . which brought sudden, frightening thoughts of the Bellevue Brothers. Would Clint want them on the wedding list? Courtney shuddered, remembering the innate evil of the two men. And, somewhere out there, she remembered suddenly, there were two other half-brothers. Were they Bellevues?

Well, this was no time to think on such things. But she did want to think about Efraim. Her older brother would be here. No court case could keep the young lawyer from giving her away. As to Mother and Vanessa . . . well, Efraim would know if they had settled in Europe after Mother's late husband made away with the Glamora fortune and brought shame to her Bellevue bloodline. Shame? Courtney wondered for the first time what Mother's reaction would be to the Washington Bellevues! Well, never mind that either.

June, the magical month, was almost here. No storm cloud could mar it, she prayed.

Chapter 2

Planning—Not Plotting

It was several days before the little handwritten notes were in the mail. One to Efraim, not newsy—just explaining that she and Clint had set the wedding date for her birthday on June thirtieth. What about Mother and Vanessa? she pondered on paper. Her brother would know. He knew almost everything. He even more than Lance Sterling—the childhood sweetheart who had vowed to win Courtney and had begun his clumsy wooing at the tender age of seven—was her idol. Until Clint! Writing to Lance had been awkward. There was no engagement to break, so she would be casual. On the other hand, how is one casual when there has been an "understanding" since their next-door-to-each-other births, if not between them, between the families? The Glamoras at the time were "monied" (unfortunate that it was new wealth—still, fortunes were not to be taken lightly). And the Sterlings, like Mother's line, were of the "aristocracy." Thank goodness there was no snobbery here on the frontier!

So it was that Courtney wrote a friendly little note:

My Dear Lance:

Since you promised to follow me here, why not make the timing to coincide with Efraim's journey? I am sure he has told you that I am being married, and nothing would please me more than to have you here for the occasion. Maybe you could even do my portrait! Nobody but you could endow me with such beauty as your charcoal sketches used to do. You always made me feel beautiful, and I needed that. I have found so many sites here for you to paint. And, of course, I am looking forward to the painting that you promised—one of Waverly Manor. I was sorry to hear that my old home was sold, but understand the circumstances that made it necessary. We will talk at length when you are here. We will arrange some time alone.

Love,

Courtney

Courtney read and reread the letter. It was unsatisfactory, but the best she could manage. How good that formality here was unheard of! In its stead were warmth and neighborliness. It would be like bringing two worlds together to introduce Efraim and Lance to the New World. As to her mother and sister . . . but such an unlikely situation would never occur.

Once the notes were dispensed with, Courtney brushed her long hair, parting it in the center as always, and strolled toward the mines where Clint would be working. Donolar must have been watching from his rose garden, and read her mind in his usual uncanny way. She had gone no more than a quarter mile when the boy galloped up beside her, leading her mare.

"You should not travel alone. I promised Clint I would take care of you. And I brought you this flower—red, the butterflies' favorite color!"

"And mine!" Courtney smiled, pinning it over her left ear to show that she was "taken," then allowing Donolar to help her mount "Peaches."

"*Mine?*" Donolar repeated Courtney's pronoun regarding the color of the rose as if it had some special significance. Then, focusing grave and expressionless eyes on hers, he said, "Yes, there's a new *arrasta* now that the other mine is being worked. I must tell the butterflies—"

"*Arrasta*, Donolar?" Courtney brought the childlike brother back to the word before it was lost. "What is that?"

"Nothing they would like, I guess. They like my roses because they speak in tongues of love. They know that the red bud you wear speaks of bashful—but true—love. But the evil ones don't know . . ."

"The *arrasta*?" Courtney prompted gently.

"No, they couldn't operate it. It takes a mule—there! See for yourself!"

They had reached the silver mines, and what Courtney saw was a revelation. A donkey—no, three of them like a carousel—were pulling a boxlike contrivance round and round a sapling pole around which were heavy, smooth rocks. The post moved with the animals, and something looking like a silver fog sifted down into containers. Courtney had limited knowledge of mining, but something told her that this contrivance took the place of panning, that the mines were doing well.

And then all such thinking faded. "*Courtney!*"

"I o'er took her, Clint—watching like you said I should!" Donolar's voice was filled with pride.

Clint murmured a thank-you and swooped Courtney from Peaches' back. "My darling, my darling—wearing a rose to show she's spoken for!" Ignoring the audience, he kissed her ear.

"Clint Desmond!" Courtney whispered shyly against the rough, sweat-soaked shirt that covered a throbbing heart.

"All right, we'll begin anew," Clint teased, his rich, male voice low and intimate. Clearing his throat, he began with mock formality.

"Miss Glamora, I believe?"

Clint stepped backward to stand a proper distance.

Courtney burst into helpless laughter. She, like him, was remembering their first words on the train under Nanny's watchful eye.

"Was I really that awful?"

"You were really that wonderful—even with soot all over that Madonna face!"

It was Courtney who covered the distance between them with one short step. Pulling herself up on tiptoe, the top of her head still reached only his wide shoulders. Tilting her face upward, she met the expected pair of blue, blue eyes— lakes, they were, and as usual she was drowning in them. The sun-bronzed hair with its rebellious kink, the clean-cut nose and the formidable strength of purpose of the jawline still fascinated her. Imagine awakening every morning and—

"Well, do I pass inspection?" Clint's voice was amused.

"Oh, darling," Courtney scolded, her pink face due more to her thoughts than to the question, "stop playing that silly game. I was young and foolish when we met on that awful train ride—"

"Two years younger than now. How," he asked the sky, "could a 22-year-old man of the world have robbed the cradle as I did?" Then, turning back to Courtney, "But I will grant you the now-wisdom of an 18-year-old—"

"As of June thirtieth."

"As of our wedding day!"

"Which *proves* that I'm wiser now. I was afraid of you then."

Clint lifted a playful hand as if to swat her. "Best you remain that way, my brazen English orphan."

"Touch me and I'll scream." Courtney was enjoying their banter enormously. She bore no resemblance to the child she had been then—a lonely little girl who had lost the father she loved and consequently had been sent away by her mother. Away from Efraim. Away from Lance. Away from "home," if one could call the manor home. And all of this so a beautiful but fickle mother could marry a money-grabbing count whose only talent was swindle. It was good enough—divine justice, one might say—that it happened. Good enough, too, that her favorite daughter, equally beautiful and fickle, would tread daintily in her footsteps.

"Why so pensive, my darling? Where did the shine go?"

"Oh," she said lightly, "don't forget 'penniless' among your adjectives." Courtney frowned at her own words. "What *do* we do about them—our mothers and siblings, I mean?"

Clint cupped her small chin in his great hand. Then he answered with just the right amount of bitterness. "We do for them what they would wish. It was they who deserted ship. I'm speaking of our mothers, who are decidedly alike! As to your brother, you have made arrangements with him— exactly as I would want you to. And your—er, friend—is he coming, too?"

Courtney colored slightly. "Yes. That is, I think so. And Clint—friend is all he is."

"Better be," Clint growled. And then they laughed together as he gathered her into his arms again. "Basically, I'm a caveman at heart and your hair would be a temptation."

Courtney, seeing that there were no curious onlookers, snuggled close. How could any girl be so lucky? No, *lucky* was the wrong word. *Blest!* It was Providence that brought them together. And it was Clint who had made her aware. Oh, how she loved them both: God in His heaven, and Clint . . . so tall . . . so lean . . . so lithe . . . without an ounce of superfluous flesh. But bursting at the seams with love and kindness.

Donolar had wandered into the Company Store for an apple. Nobody grew apples like Washington farmers and nobody kept them as polished as the Store's proprietor. Tony Bronson kept barrels of the local fruit "spit and polished" in a special section marked LOKAL PRODUSE.

Saturdays were a madhouse—the day when all the miners' wives brought their broods in to shop for a week's supply of victuals.

But Clint brought Courtney back to the moment at hand. "What brings my beautiful bride-to-be here other than to declare her love?"

Courtney drew back. "Have I done that? You are so smug!"

Clint drew her close again. "I am smug because I have the most beautiful, the most wonderful, the most people-serving lady in this beautiful valley in my arms—forever."

"First a wedding, then *forever*," Courtney murmured contentedly. But there were business matters. "About your brothers—"

"Two in prison, as you know, and the other two—who knows?"

"Are they Bellevues, Clint? I never thought it was important until now. Mother will want to know about the family—"

"Brothers, but not *family*, Courtney. And I've no more idea where they are than where I would find my mother. My family is you, Y-O-U, Aunt Bella, Donolar, Dr. Lovelace, Brother Jim and his congregation, these men—oh, Courtney, have I told you how much I love you?"

Courtney concentrated. "Not often enough," she said. "Stop—I can't talk with you holding me so close. Clint, I— well, please don't think I am making suggestions—but— have you plotted off a homestead for us? I want to start planning the house."

"And move the ancestral lineup from the library? My darling, Arabella Kennedy would have our hides! Seriously, I had planned this as a surprise—"

Clint paused and waved his hand toward the donkeys. At that moment Donolar's curly, blond head peeked cautiously from the door of the Company Store. One could never be too careful, especially without the help of the butterflies. Courtney smiled at Clint lovingly. They both adored the half-man, half-child who had been rejected by Courtney's mother.

Seeing that all was safe, Donolar emerged, biting into the most enormous apple Courtney had ever seen—undoubtedly a gift of Mr. Bronson. Donolar did not carry money, for, while he could quote any play of Shakespeare from cover to cover, he was unable to calculate in figures. Besides, wasn't money evil, like the Bellevue brothers? One could not serve God and mammon . . .

The childlike boy made a lot of sense to Courtney, but for now she must conclude the conversation before he joined them. "The *arrasta*?" she surprised Clint by questioning.

"How did you know?"

"Donolar told me and I am curious—"

Hearing his name, Donolar quickened his pace. Ever obedient, he addressed Clint, "Yessir?"

"It's all right, Donolar," Clint reassured him. "Your sister surprised me. That's all. I didn't know you'd told her—"

Donolar looked like a lovely trapped animal, too inexperienced to think his way from the jaws of some cruel trap. "I only told part—I—I never mentioned the gold—Oh! Oh my!"

Clint laughed deeply and richly. "That's all right, too. We're all one family. It's true, Courtney. We've hit a small vein."

"*Gold!*" Courtney could not believe her ears.

"Enough to let the men spin dreams. The *arrasta* is Jose's idea—something he learned during the California Gold Rush days. And I suppose you think I am dodging your question about our house?"

"You never dodged anything in your life!"

Clint's cheek against hers was her reward. She was sorry when he straightened his giant form and looked down at her. "Aunt Bella feels," he said slowly, "that we should allow the workers to stake out claims—even take the best of the building sites—since they were so faithful during the lean years when the silver mines were not paying."

How like Cousin Bella. Courtney nodded in understanding. But what of a home for themselves?

Clint, as usual, read her mind. "That is, providing you are willing to go on living in the Mansion with my aunt. We will have loads of privacy. An army could take up quarters. It is her wish, and she was going to approach you but was hesitant for fear of losing you—"

Tears sprang to Courtney's eyes. "She could never do that. Why, I would love to live there. It is to be yours anyway."

"Yours and mine—and now, my love, it's back to work or I won't be able to support you properly."

Courtney and Donolar rode back in near-silence, each buried in private thought. Courtney was remembering with great affection the great, grostesquely beautiful Mansion, its visions of the past and its dreams of the future. "Thank You, Lord," she whispered.

Chapter 3

A Special Sunday

Sundays were unfailingly ritualistic in the Mansion-in-the-Wild. The ritual did not include sleeping late. Man labored six days a week and on the seventh he honored his Maker. That honoring began very early. In fact, the entire household was up to wake the birds, Courtney decided, and behaved accordingly. Clint and Donolar gathered roses from Donolar's "Isle of Innisfree," which to her surprise bloomed almost the year round. Donolar planted the timid ones nearest to his cabin so that they bloomed out of season. Roses gathered, dew-fresh, the two men hitched the teams to two buggies. One was for the immediate "family," which included Arabella Kennedy, Clint, Courtney, and Donolar as well as Mrs. Rueben (the German housekeeper) and Mandy, whose ebony face and white-toothed smile filled the day with sunshine.

"This *is* mah day off," she was fond of saying. "De work's dun and I reckon de Lawd don' mind iffen I jest put on the finishin' touches, like pourin' de batter fer de sourdough flapjacks into de skillet—singin' hymns while dey fry."

The other buggy was for the roses and for the "extended family." Brother Jim made a practice of "just happening" to be in the neighborhood unless there was "an ox in the ditch." And Dr. Lovelace—well, he made no such pretense. He was at the long, white-clothed table—unless one of the Kennedy Silver Mines' wives decided to deliver on Sunday. That was fine too, as everybody knew that Sunday's child was blest over all others.

On the first Sunday in June all gathered around the table, where Arabella Kennedy in her inevitable long, black dress (this time softened by a white lace bertha) presided. Usually the doctor sat at the head of the table or else his chair was left vacant. But today was different. Clint and Courtney's relative-in-common put her dear friend at the opposite end, serving as host by arrangement.

Dr. Lovelace silenced all chatter by rapping sharply on his Haviland china plate. Cousin Bella winced sharply; but when there was no sound of broken glass, she relaxed while the good man explained that (*ahem*) although generally, as they all knew, only one diner asked the blessing, today was different (*ahem*), yes, very different. Each would offer a prayer, but (pulling an enormous gold watch from his vest pocket) "for goodness sake make them to the point, there being an important announcement after the last *Amen*." The group obliged.

Arabella Kennedy took her cue. "I should like to have it known," Cousin Bella began formally, lifting a frail hand and managing to look tall, "that my dear cousin, Miss Courtney Glamora, has consented to become the bride of my beloved nephew, Clinton Desmond, and (lifting her salt-and-pepper-adorned head proudly) that they will be married on June thirtieth at the little Church-in-the-Wildwood. The Reverend Brother Jim will perform the ceremony, and—"

Cousin Bella paused for breath, then continued: "And in case that Efraim, Donolar's twin brother, is unable to be so far from his Eastern home—lawyers are busy people—the honorable Doctor George Washington Lovelace will give the bride away."

Doc George pulled his rotund body from the host's chair. The dimpled hand that he ran through his cloud of white hair mingled an aroma of pills and bay rum with Donolar's centerpiece of fragrant roses. Nobody, Courtney thought as her dark eyes glowed with happiness, except the good doctor could have treated what had been common knowledge—for, well, maybe longer than she had known—as news.

"Well, now, that calls for a bit of a toast—early as it is in the morning!" Doc George said jovially. His merry blue eyes were even bluer than usual, this white-bearded Santa who dispensed homeopathic medicine and wisdom throughout the settlement, as he said: "Up with the grape juice as we drink to the health of the happy couple!"

Later Courtney Glamora was to look back on the morning as one of the happiest of her life. Nothing could have foretold the tragedy which lurked in the shadows of the great house, a tragedy about which "only the butterflies knew." Even Brother Jim, the gorilla of a man who was known for his prophecies, foresaw nothing ahead but happiness.

*   *   *

The buggy wheels hummed love songs to Courtney's ears as the family rode briskly along beneath a blue-enameled sky. Her heart beat so rapidly that at times she was sure the blood would burst through her thin, ivory skin. And Clint's great hands, which held hers, throbbed with the same rhythmic flow. *Oh, dear God, it's good to be alive*, she whispered inwardly, knowing that He would hear.

Although the church was some distance away, it appeared suddenly—a weathered little building whose disproportionately tall spire poked at the white-sheep clouds and seemed to spring from its jungle of fir trees in welcome. The group, once the horses were tethered outside, entered the building quietly. There was something so sacred about the place—the place where Courtney had given her heart to God and would give her life to Clint come her birthday— that the hobnail-scarred boards upon which they trod to seat themselves quietly might well have been marble to her feet.

With much aplomb Brother Jim marched through the worshipers who had gathered ahead of them and, eyes closed, prayed audibly. The wind-punished pines nearby joined them.

There was the usual mingling of buckskins, proper dark suits, and coonskin caps among the men and the bleak starchiness of floor-length calico dresses and matching poke bonnets among the women. Courtney was glad that she herself preferred simple clothes and that her gray silk tunic with one of Donolar's Pink Perfection rosebuds pinned on her shoulder would not embarrass the women when they heard the "news." For there could be no denying that this was Brother Jim's Big Moment. One could tell from the way he strutted, with his suit (which looked far too small for his enormous frame) threatening to split at the seams as he mounted to the hand-hewn pulpit.

She was right. The onetime prizefighter did not remove his frayed tie, as was his usual preparation for an "Is it well with thee?" sermon. And, instead of his warnings to gamblers and moonshiners, he took a beautiful detour.

"Now, folks, I've spent enough time warning the evildoers. Like Noah, I'm preparing to close the ark! It's time we talked about its destination, having bulged its ribs with the righteous. So, today instead of worrying about how we're going to get a hat on over the horns of the sinner in his eternal damnation, let's talk about the golden streets of heaven, where the Tree of Life is in eternal bloom . . . no sickness . . . no pain . . . no pesky insects . . . our only concern being how to get robes on over our wings!"

His description of heaven, straight from the book of Revelation, was electrifying. And Courtney was sure her heart would burst when he made the announcement that she and Clint were to be married. "That union's about as close to that Holy Place as you can get on this earth, folks!"

There was a chorus of *Amens*, followed by a squeaky note from the pitch pipe, and then the group was singing "When We All Get to Heaven"—which Courtney hardly heard. Then, suddenly, they were all outdoors, bruising the newly fallen pine needles. Children were tossing cones into the air in wild abandon, well aware that their parents were focusing their attention elsewhere.

The *elsewhere* was clustered around Courtney and Clint. Laughing. Crying. Pumping their hands up and down like the lever on some frozen bit of machinery. And embracing them joyously. At last the great minister pushed his way past Ahab, the smithy, Tony, of the Company Store, and countless couples whom Courtney had met when accompanying Brother Jim on his calling or Doc George Lovelace when there was an outbreak of flu.

"Make way for the leader!" the preacher boomed. "It's high time I am planting the 'holy kiss' on this bride!"

Courtney felt herself blush as he kissed her brow. She was about to murmur that she was not a bride yet when she caught sight of two strangers—the last to leave the little church.

Something about the two nattily dressed men seemed vaguely familiar, although she knew she had never met the two—except perhaps in a dream. Both had thick, dark hair like her own and eyes that, although too close together, seemed to be everywhere at once. There could be no doubt that the strong-featured, somewhat arrogant men were brothers . . . and then she knew! They were the missing Bellevues. A sense of foreboding clawed at her heart.

Chapter 4

Identity

In the busy days that followed, Courtney was wrapped in a cocoon of happiness. The only thing that took a bit of the sheen off the early-June days (in which women throughout the Washington settlement bustled about, frequenting the premises of the Mansion for quilting bees and secretive planning) was the fact that she saw too little of Clint. She joined him in wishing that there were a simpler way of getting married. Cousin Bella was shocked at their failure to recognize that their marriage was a "community affair."

"Stop building tomorrow's roads on today's grounds," she scolded gently. "You will have the rest of your lives together. Indulge the ladies for now."

And she put affectionate arms around her first cousin, Gabriel Glamora's daughter, and her nephew on the Kennedy side. Not given to affection, it was one of her rare moments of revealing the real Arabella Kennedy behind the regal air that rose above Courtney's remembered snobbery of her mother. She had grown to love this authoritative relative deeply. Perhaps some of Cousin Bella's appeal was due to her resemblance to Courtney's father (the "dark side," Mother had called it) . . . tall . . . angular . . . with midnight-black hair—threaded with silver—piled high on her head. But Courtney loved her for more than that. Her fondness was due to the fact that her spinster-cousin was soft of heart, having taken Donolar when Mother refused to rear an "idiot child," then—with the same grace— "inviting" Courtney to the Northwest Mansion when the

Lady Ana Bellevue Glamora sent her away in order to exchange her late husband's fortune and her beauty for a title that was somewhat less tarnished than her own.

On Courtney's few stolen moments with Clint she had little opportunity to ask about the two strangers who very probably were his half-brothers. Clint was too busy pouring out his visions of the future. The odds were against their finding much gold, he admitted. But his faithful men would dig and dig again. What the homesteaders plowed and sowed for the miners picked and dug for. Men were entitled to their dreams. As for himself, he had his. And he would gather Courtney tenderly in his arms for a blissful moment—a moment when neither of them cared about the world, a selfish little moment all their own . . . sacred . . . beautiful . . . blest by the Creator . . .

But most of those moments were interrupted by Donolar, who insisted that they must see that the roses were holding back their sweetest blossoms until The Day. He was so excited that there was no denying him. And once in his garden, it was impossible to escape. They must see every rose and learn its secrets. The butterflies planned it all, Donolar knew.

On one of those tours, on a bright mid-June day when anything seemed possible, it was Donolar himself who approached the topic which Courtney thought only she knew about. It was uncanny how *he* knew what he attributed to the butterflies.

"Clint," he said, raising innocent blue eyes and looking into nothingness, "they are back, aren't they?"

"Your butterflies? Yes, Donolar they're back. What news do they bring?"

Donolar's blue eyes appeared to be attempting to focus like those of a newborn baby. His round, childish face was without expression when he answered.

"I mean the other brothers."

Clint straightened from his position of examining a tightfisted white rosebud which he had been about to pick for Courtney. White was purity, Donolar had said. Now, he looked at Donolar with the appraising eyes of a stranger.

"Whatever are you talking about, Donolar? Has someone been bothering you again?"

"Not yet—but they will. Or maybe it's you. And," he promised with a solemnity that would have been comical on another person about another matter, "I will take care of Courtney, just as always. Nothing must stop your marriage—"

Clint's voice was low. "If you see strangers, you are to tell me. Do you understand? It could be important."

Donolar began babbling senselessly then about the fears of the butterflies. He was still talking to himself when Courtney and Clint turned to go. As they walked the short distance from Donolar's "Isle" to the Mansion, he behaved as if nothing were amiss. But something in his voice warned Courtney that he was worried. And she knew by his obvious surprise at Donolar's words that he had failed to see the two strangers the day their engagement was announced.

While Courtney counted the days eagerly until her wedding day (crossing each off in her "Dear God" journal for Clint), occasionally she grew weary of the constant din of voices as the women quilted and of the endless list of preparations she must make. Foremost was the simple white silk mull dress, the only trimming being a Valenciennes lace yoke and lace insertion on the three-quarter-length mutton-leg sleeves. The waist *must* be shirred to show that "waspy figgah," Mandy insisted, and Mrs. Rueben held out for clusters of wide tucks just below the shirring. The cook and housekeeper had taken over even though it was Cara Laughten (whose baby Courtney had helped Doc George deliver) who was making the gown, being the only woman in the valley to own a sewing machine. Cousin Bella had produced (quite mysteriously) a quaint lace cap, taking the seed pearls off and opting for a crown of Donolar's roses. Everyone seemed to have a "finger in the pie," according to her, but she would have the last say in arrangement of the flowers and chairs here at the Mansion for the reception.

Courtney felt a need for fresh air and sunlight. Soon she must have Cara, one of the closest neighbors, do a final fitting of the dress. But now she would rest just a moment.

So thinking, she sank wearily onto a long outside chair, letting the morning sun warm her skin as it filtered through the full-grown leaves of the maple tree, which offered full shade in the afternoon. Such a beautiful day, she thought lazily. The blue camas had given way to wild-apple blossoms, and laurel bloomed victoriously in the hills. The season had brought no more changes than those in Courtney's heart. Could any prospective bride be happier now that the "evil ones" (as Donolar called Clint's older half-brothers) had been incarcerated and Alexis Worthington Villard was out of his life for good? At the thought of the flaming-haired beauty with the slash of red that formed the insolent mouth, Courtney's heart beat a little faster. She had made it so clear that Clint was hers, but Courtney refused to let her mind linger on that part of the past, dismissing the chapter as she had dismissed the hurts of her childhood. She looked ahead to a future as bright as the sunlight which was nurturing Donolar's garden. Thinking of her brother brought Courtney to wonder just how much, if anything more, he knew of the two Bellevue brothers, for there was no doubt in her mind that this was who they were.

The thought made her a little uneasy. Besides, there were things to be accomplished. But first a short walk. Whenever she left the house, she generally told Cousin Bella; but this day she felt a need to feel alone, if only for a moment.

She passed through the little grove of fir trees which strove to hide the Mansion, and stood on a rise which gave her a full view of the rich valley. Concentrating on the wild, sparsely-populated beauty of it and the Mighty Hand in control, Courtney failed to hear the two riders whose steeds trod noiselessly over the cushion of dead fir needles.

"Why, if it isn't Miss Glamora. Good morning, Cousin Courtney!"

Courtney jumped at the sound of the man's voice. Even as she whirled in surprise, she recognized the pair immediately as being the men she had seen at church.

Stifling the desire to scream as the men dismounted, Courtney managed to say, "I don't believe we've met."

Indeed, she would have fled had they not stood between her and the path which had brought her here. But, trapped, she listened wordlessly as the nattily dressed pair told her that they were on the way to the mines. She never remembered responding but did manage a faint farewell. Then she all but ran through the grove and into the sunlit yard of home.

Courtney was too shaken to repeat the incident to Cousin Bella. And she was still distraught at dinner. Fortunately, Clint was late. All others were present.

Clint arrived as Doc George was carving the duck. And, after being properly welcomed, he said quietly, "I have some news which I think should be shared. It may mean little—or—"

"Yes?" Cousin Bella prompted when his voice faltered.

"Milton and Horace showed up today—my missing half-brothers. And," he inhaled deeply, "Milton has married Alexis."

Chapter 5

Shattering News

Cara bent down, her head nearly touching the floor of the rough boards of the Laughten cabin, careful not to disturb the basted folds of Courtney's wedding dress. With practiced skill Cara picked at a tiny thread at the bottom of the skirt, which stood out daintily like an inverted mushroom.

"Stand still now 'til I draw th' thread clear 'round t' make sure it's even."

Courtney stood very still as the white thread obediently yielded to Cara's gentle tug. She was biting it off with pearly teeth, her hair falling limply around her face, when there was a knock at the door.

"Quick-like, git yourself into the bedroom. Could be the boss man, and it would be bad luck if he was to see you in this getup before you meet him at the altar."

Courtney smiled in amusement but did as she was told. It was a matter of pride that the miners' wives disliked having their superstitions questioned. She had little more than closed the crude door behind her when Cara whispered through the crack in a frightened voice.

"Miz Glamora—"

"Courtney!"

"Courtney, hon, they's three Chinamen out front 'n I cain't understand a word they're sayin' and—"

Without listening for another word, Courtney pushed open the door and, forgetting the fragility of the wedding dress, hurried to the small porch, a certain *knowing* gripping her heart. It would be the three workmen who came to tell Clint of the explosion of the mine two years ago even though he was not fully recovered from pneumonia. It was a bad omen that they should show up again . . . or was she being superstitious too?

Courtney stared at the men wordlessly, feeling the blood drain from her heart. Some distant part of her wondered vaguely if Americans of European descent looked as ridiculously alike to Orientals as these men looked to her with their moon-skinned faces bobbing up and down as they spoke between themselves in high-pitched, musical voices. The other part of her knew instinctively that something had happened—something for which they were trying desperately to find words. She would have to help.

"Mr. Desmond—Clint—?" she managed weakly.

Upon hearing her voice, the three stopped in unison and turned expressionless faces toward her. Then, bowing low, they began talking nonstop in their native tongue.

Courtney lifted a restraining hand and shook her head, hoping that the gesture indicated that she understood nothing. Apparently it did, because she could sense a meshing of gears as they in turn attempted to communicate.

At length the man in the middle said, "Ees velly—"

"Seek," offered the worker to his right. But the one to his left was shaking his head, causing his cue to bounce comically. "No ees seek—ees—" and from his gestures around his face, Courtney guessed at the word.

"Injured—hurt?" she whispered faintly.

In unison they agreed: "Boss man hurted—velly hurted."

"Where—is—Clint—your boss?" she spaced each word carefully. "At the mine?"

When their identical heads shook furiously, Courtney tried again. "Where—*where* is your boss—at the mine?"

Again, the shaking and then, as if inspired, the man in the middle whirled and pointed past their rickety buckboard and toward the Mansion.

Deaf ears did not hear Cara's calls for Courtney to come back, to change her dress. Courtney lifted her unhemmed skirt and raced through the brambles, feeling them clutch at the thin fabric, then thinking that it mattered little. She might never be wearing it after all.

At the door, a pale Arabella Kennedy stopped Courtney with a command. "Calm yourself, my child. The *arrasta* sprang apart, injuring some of the men. Now get upstairs and get changed. The doctor is with Clint. Donolar is meeting them and we must be prepared for any eventuality."

Courtney paused before obeying. "It's bad, isn't it?"

"It's bad," replied Cousin Bella.

Chapter 6

A World of Darkness

Courtney never remembered tearing at the silk mull of her wedding gown, letting it slip carelessly to the floor, and getting herself buttoned into a pink shirtwaist cotton dress. Her thoughts were with Clint and the men who were bringing him home. Down the hall she could hear Mrs. Rueben and Mandy as they prepared his room. Maybe they needed a hand; but, no, she must run back downstairs to keep vigil with Cousin Bella.

Joining her at the window by the front door, Courtney slipped a trembling hand into the older woman's hand. Cousin Bella's fingers tightened around hers painfully hard.

"He's alive, Courtney. That's all that counts."

Courtney nodded, wishing she could cry. Tears were the balm of the heart. But there were no tears—just the malignant fear that the tragedy was worse than they could imagine. The grandfather clock chimed the hour of ten and the cuckoo clock in the library upstairs echoed the call. It seemed to Courtney that they had waited for hours when actually it could have been no more than minutes.

"There they are!" Cousin Bella barely controlled herself.

Courtney, who had been unable to find a voice, let go of her cousin's hand and rushed toward the door. With hands that fumbled she finally found the knob, and, in spite of protests from Cousin Bella as well as Mrs. Rueben and Mandy, who had heard the announcement and rushed down the stairs, she bounded to meet the group of men carrying Clint on a litter. At least, she supposed it was Clint. His head was so swathed in bandages that it was hard to tell.

Courtney was dimly aware of the men's identity. Doc George, one hand on Clint's pulse and the other swinging his inevitable black bag, stood close to the litter which four men were bearing. Their clothes were bloodstained and their faces resembled those of pallbearers—telling Courtney more than words.

With a slow, steady gait—so as to do no further injury to the patient—the men marched in studied rhythm. Donolar . . . Brother Jim (who was chanting a prayer and barking orders simultaneously) . . . and the Bellevues. The Bellevues? At any other time Courtney would have pondered on their presence. She could only think with a single cell of her brain: *So they are not responsible.* The rest of her was with Clint in whatever unconscious world he occupied.

"Upstairs!" Arabella Kennedy ordered quietly. Mrs. Rueben and Mandy stood fastened to the floor.

To and fro . . . to and fro . . . were the stairs endless? Courtney wondered as she trailed with leaden feet behind them.

When at last they reached the top, Doc George let go of Clint's wrist and put a kindly, dimpled hand on her arm.

"Go back downstairs, my dear—"

"But I can't—" she whispered. "I have to be with him—he'll be asking for me—"

"Not for awhile, Courtney. Now be a good girl and do as I tell you. Conserve your strength, as you will be sorely needed when I have him patched together. Right now Clint's in shock—unconscious—and in need of help that only the Lord and I can give him."

"Is there *nothing* I can do?"

"You can pray—pray that he's not blind."

"*Blind!*" The single word seemed to explode and fall in broken shards at her feet. "Oh, dear God, he *can't* be—"

The men had already entered Clint's room and closed the door. Courtney turned slowly and, gripping the banister, made her way down the stairs to where the others waited to comfort her. They brought coffee, which she refused. They said soothing words, which she did not hear. And they tried to coax her to lie down in the sunroom. But Courtney walked woodenly and stood looking out the window wordlessly.

Blind. Clint could be blind. He might live in a world of darkness in which he would never see his beloved Dream Country again. At last, with a little cry, she began to beat her chest in hopeless desperation, feeling herself sinking . . . sinking . . . then being caught up by loving arms and laid on a couch. There she too succumbed to a world of darkness.

Chapter 7

The Vigil

Awake moments later, Courtney sprang up. She reached the bottom of the stairs and sat down, her small body curled into a fetal-ball shape, and—with hands covering her face—moaned as she swayed back and forth pitifully. In shock herself, she was oblivious of the subdued voices raised in prayer, the softened treads in the kitchen where Mandy was preparing "soul food," and the little breeze that crept in from the open window to lift her hair playfully and cool her burning forehead. How long did it take for a doctor to determine whether the patient would see?

When at last she heard the faint squeak of Clint's door opening slowly, she jerked herself erect and bounded up the stairs, stumbling over the pink skirt she had forgotten to lift. At the landing Doc George stopped her, his rotund body barring the way. Dropping his bag, he gripped her shoulders.

"Move over!" Courtney cried. "Let go of me! I *have* to be with Clint—don't you understand?"

"Indeed, I do," the doctor said kindly. "You'll be the best medicine—in time. But for now, there must not be the slightest noise. Even a footstep could undo my work."

Doctor George Washington Lovelace did not relax his grip. "Courtney, listen to me, little one," he whispered. "You're a born nurse. You demonstrated that when you nursed Clint back to health in that bout with pneumonia, and over and over as you visited sick folk with me. Soon now you will be taking over here, but not now. Be a good girl—come into the sunroom with me—and I will explain his condition. Believe me, I know what's best for him."

Courtney believed him. She reached out one small hand of submission and allowed herself to be led down the stairs.

In the sunroom, Doc George shooed the others away. "I will tell all of you the story in time. But for now may Courtney and I be alone?"

Quietly the men who had carried the litter set down their coffee cups and went out through the front door. Cousin Bella followed them, ever the serene hostess—even though her nephew and light of her life lay blinded upstairs. Courtney marveled at the woman's calm and drew courage from it.

Doc George pulled out a chair for her. Obediently she sat down and maintained her silence.

"I'm not sure how it happened. Just one of those freak accidents—no foul play, as far as I can determine. The best the excited workers could tell me was that the bucket on the *arrasta* tilted and flung crushed rock at breakneck speed mostly in the direction of Clint. He sustained a few lacerations—that kind of thing—but—"

When he paused, Courtney said tonelessly, "Go ahead, please."

Doc George characteristically ran stubby fingers through his cloud of white hair. "Are you sure you are up to this?"

"I am up to it."

"Yes. Yes, I guess you are," he said, laying an appreciative hand on hers, which were knotted in her lap. "First, how much do you know about the human eyeball?"

"Not much," Courtney admitted.

"Well," he hesitated, uncertain where to begin, "there are several principal parts of the eyeball, among them being the cornea, the choroid, and the retina—"

"Which part was damaged?"

"I'm not certain—not *dead* certain—but why don't I just tell you in simple terms what happened? The—"

For the first time, expression came back to Courtney's dark eyes and the doctor smiled. "Good sign," his always-twinkling eyes seemed to say, pleased when her color heightened. She spoke with agitation, "How long will he be blind? Will he be able to see when the bandages are off? Today? Tomorrow? *Soon?*"

"Wait a minute—whoa now—you must listen to me. I can't answer that. I've a lot of reading up to do. First, let me tell you what I know for sure and what I've done about it. I have sutured the lacerations—"

"One eye or two?" Courtney waited breathlessly.

"Both, I'm afraid. But as far as I am able to determine—and this is just a shot in the dark—the corneas are all right. Better pray about that one. But the whites were a mess—more lacerations than barnacles on a ship. I had to do surgery up there, suturing what I could bring together—then brought the membranes down for protection—"

"It sounds awful," Courtney shuddered, more frightened than she had ever been before in her life. "He *will* see?" The question came out piteously.

"Only God in His heaven knows that, and even He will take His time in revealing it. We won't know until the bandages are off—like two weeks from now—but I am going to the Fort's pharmacy in search of some special drops to keep the bandages soaked. I will be back tonight—"

"Can I see him then?" Courtney interrupted, knowing full well that it would do no good to wheedle for a sooner time. When his nod came, she asked the dread question.

"What can I do? I will do anything—*anything*—"

"You can catch catnaps like a good girl and eat to get some meat on those little bones. You're going to need your strength. And something else: Be sure that nobody, *nobody* enters that darkened room. He's sedated, and I want him to sleep until I return. Understand?"

Courtney nodded numbly. The doctor patted her shoulder and went to explain to the others while her lonely vigil began.

Chapter 8

Painful Visit

Refusing dinner, Courtney remained in the sunroom, her eyes riveted to the trail which would bring Doc George, watching the evening sun dip dangerously low. He had promised to be back and to let her see Clint. But if he waited much longer, a visit from either of them would be impossible. There could be no light . . . no parting of the drapes . . . no lighting of a lamp . . . nothing but the total world of darkness in which Clint lived both in his room and behind the bandages.

Only occasionally did she dare take her eyes off the road, and that was to tiptoe upstairs and listen for the faintest sound from Clint's bedroom. When there was none, she would hurry back to her watching place. She was sorely tempted to slip into the room and check on Clint herself. But, remembering the doctor's cautions, she refrained.

So, as she watched, she prayed, "Please, Lord, let the doctor come before dark—how thankful I am for the long twilights. And please, Lord, *please* let Clint's eyes allow him to see these twilights again—if it is Your will—"

It was in the middle of one of her ambiguous prayers that Courtney saw Doc George's ancient hack. With a small cry of joy she flung open the door and ran to meet him.

"Did you get them—the medicine drops? May I go in with you, Doc George? What did you learn from the medical book?"

Courtney was taking the reins and the doctor's bag as he climbed down from the hack. Then, waiting for answers and hardly daring to breathe, she handed the reins to Donolar, who had appeared out of nowhere.

"Thank you, Donolar," Doc George said, and then to Courtney, "and you, young lady, give a man a chance to catch his breath. I have the medicine. I learned a great deal from the quick scan I had time to give the case. And, yes, you may be able to see Clint—but not until after I do. Now, go tell the others I am here and let me go up alone."

It seemed an eternity before he appeared at the landing and curled a finger in invitation to Courtney, then put a cautioning finger to his lips for silence. Cousin Bella, Mrs. Rueben, Mandy, and Donolar stood in a silent row as Courtney, lifting her skirts this time to increase her speed, rushed up the stairs to meet the doctor, and together they ascended the second flight.

At Clint's door, Doc George stopped. "If you have a needle and thread in your room, go get it while I check to see if he's awake. I gave him tincture of opium."

Threaded needle in hand, Courtney waited for the doctor to open Clint's door. When at last the door opened with the familiar squeak, Courtney entered the gray darkness of the shadowy room. Wordlessly the doctor took the needle from Courtney's hand and motioned her to the other side of the bed as he knelt beside Clint.

"We'll only stay long enough for me to stitch on these bandages," Doc George whispered, "unless the patient awakens—and you'd better pray that he doesn't. He's going to be in terrible pain."

Courtney nodded numbly and eased herself to the side of the bed opposite where the doctor worked. When at last her eyes adjusted to the semidarkness, what she saw was appalling. The bandages that covered Clint's head, stopping just below his nose, were blood-soaked. The rest of his face was swollen beyond recognition and had turned a strange purplish-blue.

"Internal bleeding," Doc George whispered as he secured the bandages with thread, knotted it, and clipped both ends.

But Courtney, who was on her knees, was paying little attention now to what she had seen. Instead, another fear gripped her heart—one far greater than the fear of Clint's blindness. He was breathing in shallow gasps—gasps so feeble that his chest scarcely swelled the quilt which covered him. Supposing . . . oh, dear God, just *supposing* . . . Clint did not *live* . . .

Courtney's lips moved in disjointed prayer that the Lord would not let this tragedy happen to them. For how long she did not know. She was only aware of the doctor's strong hands on her shoulders . . . lifting her to her feet . . . leading her away. Sleep. Clint must sleep, he said.

In the hallway the doctor was warm and fatherly but also firm. "You *have* to get some rest. Clint will remain sedated for several hours. Try to rest until then."

"I want to be with him *now*. Every moment counts—"

"He's better off alone, Courtney," he said gently.

Courtney allowed herself to be steered downstairs, where the rest of the household waited. Doc George helped her into a chair and then addressed the pale-faced group.

"Courtney can fill you in on the details. It's a miracle that Clint Desmond is alive, is all that I can say. One man was killed, and Big Jimbo's with the family—"

"*Killed?*" The tremulous voice belonged to Donolar.

"Killed," the doctor repeated. "Several men have broken limbs, and I must get to them. The rig fell on them, but Clint took the brunt of the shards—in his eyes—"

"Is the damage permanent?" Cousin Bella's voice was almost steady, her manner practical.

Her lifelong friend sighed. "Would to God that I knew, but I am only a country doctor. It will be several weeks before I can tell. Meantime, I want somebody with him 24 hours a day. Courtney will show you the medication I have laid out for him—drops to keep the bandages soaked and something for the pain. *Soak* those bandages in spite of his protests, but don't *touch* them or allow him to. It can mean the difference between—" he paused as if unable to get the words out, and then finished the diagnosis, "—normal vision—and total blindness."

"Chicken broth—that's what Mistah Clint'll be askin' fo'," Mandy said quickly with tears streaming down her face.

"That would be good to begin with, Mandy, and then he can resume a normal diet."

"I help with—how you say, lin-*een*?" Mrs. Rueben offered in her broken English.

"Oh, that reminds me—do *not* change the sheets, Mrs. Rueben. I repeat, he must lie perfectly still. One move could undo it all. No noise. And, needless to say, no company. He will scratch and tear at the bandages, but don't allow it! Sedate him, hold him down, *anything*. And now, I must go to the others. I'll be back tomorrow—"

There were soft farewells. Then Cousin Bella saw him to the door. "God go with you, George Washington. You will be up all night, but so will we. I'll have your breakfast waiting."

Courtney slipped up the stairs. In her room, she sank wearily on her bed, still fully clothed. If there were the faintest sound from Clint she would hear.

She must have dozed, for Efraim and Lance were insisting that there was to be a wedding. They were right, but the timing was wrong. Clint's eyes were bandaged and he would be unable to see his way to the altar. The Bellevue brothers floated in. No company . . . they must leave . . . oh, no, they protested, they were here to assist Clint down the aisle . . .

There was a faint moan. "Clint!" Courtney sprang up . . .

Chapter 9

Awakening

With a pounding heart, Courtney turned the knob of Clint's door, fumbling in the darkness, and made her way to where she thought the bed should be. On the way she stumbled over a chair but managed to right herself without falling. She felt for the bed and thankfully felt the quilt yield beneath her hands.

"Clint? Clint darling?"

She sat down carefully on the edge of the bed. Clint did not answer, but she felt him stir and heard the low moan that escaped his lips.

Then, to her surprise, Clint spoke. "Where—where am I?" His voice was weak and pain-filled.

"Oh, my darling, you are home—in your own room." In the darkness she felt for his forehead and stroked it tenderly, being careful not to disturb the bandage covering it.

"You must sleep now," she whispered, feeling in the darkness for one of the powders the doctor had left. Now for a glass. The water pitcher. A spoon. Somehow she would manage. If only she could get Clint to swallow the medicine.

Her hands trembled as she tried to fit the glass beneath the mouth of the pitcher. She was unsuccessful and the water glass tilted, filling her lap with water. In a moment her clothing was soaked and she heard the *drip*, *drip* that said it had reached the floor. So this was what it was like to be blind! Overcome with frustration, Courtney waited a moment, then tried again. This time there was no spill.

Carefully she opened the square of paper holding the medicine which would ease Clint's pain, then stirred it round and round in the glass. She could only hope it was dissolved.

At last she had the potion ready. "Don't move, darling," she said soothingly to Clint. "I am going to spoon this into your mouth—"

"What?" The question was so weak that Courtney could scarcely hear it. She was sure Clint knew of a presence in the room but had not yet regained consciousness to the point of knowing who.

"It's water, Clint. The doctor says you need it so you won't dehydrate—and there's something in it to help you sleep—that's it, darling, now swallow for me!"

Clint swallowed, then swallowed again between little animalish moans of pain. She had no more than emptied the glass than he relaxed beneath the one arm that Courtney had used to support his head. His even breathing said he was sleeping.

Courtney sat rigidly beside Clint throughout the night, thankful that he did not stir. As the first gray fingers of dawn clawed the sky, Doc came as he promised.

Stiffly, Courtney eased herself from the chair, massaged the back of her neck briefly, and tiptoed across the room to open the door, praying that the squeak would not disturb Clint. Downstairs she could hear the comforting domestic sounds of pots and pans being handled gingerly so as not to disturb Clint, and, as the door yielded quietly to her touch, the smell of frying bacon wafted up the stairway ahead of Doc George's nose.

"You haven't slept!" Courtney exclaimed, seeing the rings of fatigue that rimmed his eyes.

"Neither have you—but, first, let's have a look at the patient and then we'll dig into that breakfast Bella is overseeing."

There was no talk as Doc George checked the bandages —nodding in appreciation when he saw that they were wet—and checked Clint's pulse, then turned his white-bearded face to one side as he leaned down to listen to his chest.

At last he seemed satisfied as he pointed toward the door. Courtney knew there was no need in protesting. The doctor would see that she had a decent meal if he had to haul her downstairs bodily.

A million questions filled her mind. But Doc George was praising her for a job well done and practically pushing her into the sunroom, where Cousin Bella had ordered a table set up. Dear Cousin Bella. Wise, as always. She knew that the dining room would be a grim reminder that Clint was missing.

Donolar seated Courtney as Doc George pulled out a chair for Cousin Bella. Mandy and Mrs. Rueben brought mountains of sourdough biscuits and platters of sunny-side-up eggs (the doctor's favorite method)— surrounded by crisp fingers of bacon. Then came the coffee, strong enough, it seemed, to melt the cups! Once the honey and butter were placed on the starched white cloth, the two women sat down.

"This morning, may I suggest that we—being in common agreement as to the petition we will offer—just bow our heads in silent prayer?" Cousin Bella said. And it was she who said the first "Amen."

Courtney was not hungry. She was too weary to think of the food she toyed with; but the doctor ate voraciously. He was the only man Courtney knew who seemed to know no limitations on food and not be softened by it. The only person, too, who would stuff himself and manage to talk at the same time without losing his dignity.

She listened as he repeated what he had said the day before—adding to it that he felt the danger of pneumonia was past—and then gave his prognosis. Chances were good that Clint's vision would be restored . . . still, he only *trusted* the Almighty . . . he did not possess His all-seeing eye . . .

As the sun slipped over the mountains, lining the trees with molten gold and pushing a retinue of shadows over the valley, Courtney was busy weighing and reweighing Clint's chances. It took several tries for her to hear the doctor addressing her—and longer still for her to absorb what he was saying.

"Now, I've every hope that all's well. But bear in mind I only stitched the top layer of the sclera. Hard telling how deep those lacerations go . . . Courtney, little one, best postpone the wedding . . ."

Chapter 10

Realization

For the next five days Clint was in shock—as, in a sense, was Courtney. She wondered how much, if anything, penetrated through his dark world of pain and bandages—or if indeed he understood anything at all. If not, perhaps it was God's blessing—His way of allowing Clint to suffer no more than he could bear. He was not ready, in her mind, to face the truth. And neither was she. So thinking, Courtney pushed away the terrible possibilities of what *might* be and instead lived in a gray world of her own making to protect herself from pain.

The others came and went silently, their eyes bright with unshed tears. Mandy brought broth, which Courtney tried to force between Clint's clenched teeth just before giving him the medicine which would push him into complete sleep. Mrs. Rueben offered to dust, an offer which Courtney refused, as the dust might bother Clint. Anyway, the fewer footsteps the better. Cousin Bella came in, often in the darkest hours of the night, to sit with Courtney—and their hands would lace together in silent prayer. And Donolar brought fresh roses daily, often quoting lines from Wordsworth and waiting for her to whisper their identity. The verse that made her weep was:

> To her fair words did Nature link
> The human soul that through me ran;
> And much it grieved my heart to think
> What man has made of man.

What an understanding heart God had blest the boy with! *Boy?* Donolar was no boy . . . he was Efraim's twin, which made him older than herself . . . older than Vanessa. Yes, like Efraim, he was her older brother . . .

Brother! At the thought of the word Courtney sat straight up in her vigil on the fourth night. Efraim would be on his way. With him would be Lance, on the way to her wedding—the wedding the doctor had said must be postponed. Full realization came to Courtney then. Her world had spun out of orbit with Clint's accident. And there was no way to let the two who were so close to her know. It wasn't as if she could rise and make an announcement, as Brother Jim had said he would do to the congregation come Sunday. No, they would come and there would be no wedding. "Oh, dear God, help me," she whispered.

The curtains of her mind parted then, and Courtney saw the unfinished, thorn-snagged white silk mull wedding dress . . . her long list of last-minute preparations for the wedding-that-was-not-to-be . . . and her journal. She had been unable to make entries into it daily now, so it might as well be destroyed. But *no!* her heart cried out. That would be like canceling the marriage completely, not just postponing it. And besides, in a very real sense the journal belonged to the Lord with its "Dear God" beginnings, its promises and prayers.

Thought of her brother brought Courtney to thought of Clint's. Recollection came now that the Bellevue brothers had aided with bringing Clint to the Mansion. Ordinarily she would have been frightened and shocked, and would have sought out Cousin Bella to ask the *why* of their presence. But, in her state of shock, it seemed unimportant. They could have been friendly neighbors. Even now, when she first remembered, the Bellevues seemed but small figures, bits of the past, drifting in and out of recollection. And yet they were not. What were they doing at the mine? She must talk to Cousin Bella at once . . .

Clint stirred and began mumbling about the *arrasta* . . . how it must be kept in running order . . . words of endearment to her as if everything were normal . . . and then Alexis . . .

Courtney reached for the medication, at the same time straining her ears for Clint's words. Somebody had to be in charge . . . in charge (weaker) . . . in charge . . . did Courtney know that Milt had married Alexis . . . but Horace . . . Horace . . .

With practiced hands that no longer trembled, Courtney spooned the medicine into Clint's mouth, then soaked the bandages with the all-important solution. All the while her head was spinning. What, if anything, did Clint's mumblings mean? But she pushed all questions behind in her relief that he was showing more strength. Surely that was a good sign.

She did, however, resolve that she would have a talk with Cousin Bella, and perhaps even go to the mines herself. She was about to doze when she realized that this was Sunday, the day Brother Jim would announce the postponement. Postponement . . . that's all it was. Why then the strange foreboding in her heart?

Chapter 11

What Chance Have I?

Courtney and Doc George were alone with Clint when he came out of shock completely. The doctor had (with some persuasion) convinced Cousin Bella that the family should be on hand when Big Jimbo told the disappointing news. It was only proper that Arabella and Donolar be there to receive expressions of sympathy, answer questions, and stamp out any rumors that the announcement might make. Halfheartedly Arabella consented, as did Mandy and Mrs. Rueben after being reminded somewhat grimly that nobody worked on the Lord's Day, neither the mistress "nor thy manservant, nor thy maidservant . . ."

It happened so quickly. The doctor was routinely checking Clint's pulse and nodding to Courtney when suddenly Clint jerked his arm away and, like a madman, began tearing at the wet bandages which swathed his head.

"My eyes!" he screamed. "Something is wrong with my eyes—they burn like coals of fire in my head!"

Instinctively Courtney flew to the side of the bed opposite Doc George, each grabbing an arm to restrain him.

"Don't move!" The doctor's voice was a command. "You could undo all I've done, and heaven knows I've tried to preserve your sight—"

"Courtney? I thought you were here—oh! the pain—"

"I am here, darling—right here where I belong—and I understand about the pain. Try and lie still while Doc George explains."

Clint lay still, only his ragged breathing betraying the pain, as the doctor pieced together the story as it was told to him. Then he went to great length to tell Clint of his condition and what he had done about it.

"I'll do my best to bring you through this, Clint," Doc George concluded, "but you'll have to cooperate by lying still and doing exactly as you're told."

"How long?" Clint's whisper was not one of resignation.

"Another week anyhow—and you are not to disturb the bandages. It could mean the difference."

Clint jerked away from them and tried to sit up in bed, only to be pushed firmly back down by the doctor. "I've warned you, Clint. Why not make it easier on us all?"

"There's something you're holding back. Am I going to be blind? I can take it better now than later. *Will I see?*"

Intuitively Courtney knew that the doctor felt the odds might slant in that direction. But his voice was determinedly reassuring: "That's what we're planning on, the Lord and me!"

"If I'm all right, why can't I get up, get a breath of air?"

"I didn't say you were all right," Doc George growled. "And you won't be unless you improve that humor, my lad! Either you stay put or chances are good that you'll start hemorrhaging. If that happens—"

"I won't see again?"

"Probably not. It's up to you. I'm leaving you in Courtney's charge. One bad report from this young lady and I'll finish the job the *arrasta* started."

"I'm terrified," Clint mumbled as the doctor took his leave to check on the other injured men in order to join the family when they returned from church.

Yes, Clint was terrified—but not more than Courtney. Yet his terror was not of the doctor. It, like her own, was due to the prognosis.

"If—if that happens, Courtney—where are you? If that happens," he continued as she took his hand reassuringly, "I'll be as helpless as a baby—"

"It isn't going to happen," Courtney said staunchly.

"But if it does—"

"Oh, darling," she whispered, kneeling by his side, "*I will be your eyes*. Here, feel this," she said holding the ring finger out and forcing him to trace its shape by guiding his hand. "What is it?"

"Your engagement ring, the pearl," he groaned.

"And this?" This time she extended the silver cross.

"Your birthday gift—saying 'God is love'—oh, Courtney what chance have I?"

Chapter 12

Unwelcome Guest

Courtney knew that the remaining week before the bandages were to be removed were like being in a prison cell to Clint. It took prayer for patience to help him through the alternate moods of depression and the tirades of frustration. When he threshed from side to side, Courtney was frightened.

"Darling," she implored, "you mustn't! Your eyes have to be kept level. Just pretend that you are looking straight ahead—"

"I can't pretend anymore," he said desperately.

"Soon you won't be pretending. We'll walk side-by-side, you and I, viewing the beautiful countryside."

"Courtney, listen to me! You've got to stop being so encouraging. There *are* such things as blind people."

Courtney's heart gave a lurch. How well she knew! And Clint had said of her the same thing she had thought about Doc George on occasion. Maybe they were giving false hope. But then she shook herself mentally. *Oh, thou of little faith!*

When Clint tried to turn his head again, Courtney knew she must use some ingenuity and persuasion.

"Darling, listen to me! Our future depends on how well you cooperate. Now lie still. I'm going to put a pillow on each side of your head as wedges—"

"Over my ears?" He moaned. "That way I'll be deaf as well as blind—no!"

"*Yes!*" Already Courtney was boxing in Clint's head.

"Oh, Courtney, you've been so wonderful—so sweet—and me—what have I to offer?"

"Stop the self-pity," Courtney said gently. "You have something very precious to offer me—just your love."

Clint did not answer, but she could see the muscles tighten in his jaw. With gentle fingers she stroked the spasms away and continued stroking until he was fast asleep.

Downstairs, Cousin Bella said, "Child, I declare you're as pale as a moonless night. I'm going to go up and stay with my nephew, and you're going to get out of this tomb for a few minutes. Now don't be as argumentative as the man you're going to marry. Do as I say."

Cousin Bella's crisp black skirts were already rustling on the stairway. She was right, as always. Courtney could use some air.

A few minutes later she fastened the great gate behind her and turned east toward the bluff that she and Clint loved to stand on so they could look down over the verdant valley where the little streams, forming natural irrigation, coiled and foamed until they reached the Columbia River or detoured to become little tributary waterfalls.

Once there, she breathed deeply of the pine-scented air and, feeling herself relax, allowed her eyes to wander across the mosaic of varicolored pasturelands dotted with sheep and cattle. Then her eyes climbed the foothills to where the mountains stretched darkly green to the timberline. There they met head-on with jagged rocks which seemed to touch the sun-lined clouds. How beautiful it was, this land which Providence had designed for man! Clint had shown her its wonders and, seeing it through his eyes, she had loved it immediately. Now, it seemed, she might be called upon to do the same for him. Well, God would help her . . .

Standing there motionless, Courtney was unaware that she was a study in earth tones, her ivory satin skin complementing the dark eyes and hair. Even the dress she wore today was fawn color. Totally unaware of the "study in oils" (as well as the fact that she was beautiful at all), Courtney did not notice that another's eyes were very much aware. The figure of a man had slipped from the shadows of the rock and stood dangerously close.

Courtney sensed rather than saw the man and felt a familiar coppery taste of fear fill her mouth. Too late she knew she should not have come here alone.

"Cousin Courtney, don't let me startle you."

"It seems to me you enjoy doing that," Courtney said coldly as she turned to face Milton Bellevue, "and please address me as Miss Glamora."

Milton Bellevue's closely spaced eyes narrowed into slits. "As you wish," he said with a shrug, "but aren't you a little curious as to why I followed you here?"

"I have nothing to say to you. Please leave me alone."

"I'm afraid I can't do that, Cousin—Miss Glamora. You see, you and I have some business to attend to. That is, assuming you are in charge now that my brother's blind."

"He is only temporarily indisposed—and there is nothing that you and I need to talk about. Please go."

"As you wish—although I was hoping you and I could reach an understanding as to who is in charge. Otherwise, I must see Clint Desmond myself."

Courtney hoped her voice was under control when she answered. "If you know anything at all about Clint's condition, you know that he's unable to have company. And I fail to see what business you have with him."

Milton Bellevue picked up a twig and snapped it. The small sound seemed to echo against the canyon walls, reminding Courtney of how alone she was with this man.

"I will take only a moment of your precious time, my dear. You are aware that I married Alexis Worthington—

not exactly your best friend—" his voice was a sneer which Courtney ignored. "My bumbling brothers before us got themselves in jail. I am wiser. You see, my wife retained the rights to gold, which I understand is being mined. We must reach a business agreement."

Courtney's mind did a quick flash-forward. How good it would be to have Efraim here! Being schooled in law as he was, her brother would be able to interpret all the fine print of any agreement or law that gave rights to any other than Cousin Bella and Clint.

Aloud, she said, "If you wish to discuss what you call your wife's claim, please see Miss Kennedy. I do not handle any of the business affairs. And, please, let's terminate this point-less talk."

Courtney never remembered exactly how she managed to escape. Perhaps she ran past, for she was breathless when she entered the mansion. Cousin Bella opened the door and immediately observed her agitation.

"Clint awoke. We talked a little, but he kept asking for you. Wait a minute—you can't go up there like this. What is it, my dear? What happened to upset you?"

Courtney blurted out the entire story. Then, drained, she sat waiting. It was some time before Arabella Kennedy spoke.

"I knew about this, Courtney. Clint told me. It seems that Horace and Milton Bellevue have spent quite some time at the mines—Milton trying to get his finger into the pie—and, well, Horace does not seem to be involved. In fact, he has offered to work for Clint. Both of us have our doubts as to his sincerity. But we must not judge. However, Alexis Worthington Villard Bellevue is not welcome in this house. And neither is her husband. We both know what they are!"

Chapter 13

One Moment of Hope

The long-awaited moment had arrived. The required two weeks had passed and Clint's bandages were to come off. The entire household was up before dawn, and Doc George arrived as if lured by the smell of strong coffee and sage sausage.

Courtney took only coffee. She had been unable to sleep—her mind was filled with excitement at one moment and clouded by doubt at another. The two weeks had seemed like two years and had been fraught with problems she knew needed to be settled and concerns over which she had no control. She waited for Clint to make mention of his brothers. When he did not, she avoided the subject for fear of upsetting him. And then there were Efraim and Lance to think about. For one thing, they were late in arriving—due, she learned, to travel's uncertainty.

It was about the railroads (possibly to avoid the task before him) that Doc George talked this morning, yanking at his white muttonchops as he buttered biscuits.

"Good that there were so many donations after Villard went bankrupt," he observed. "Guess you've all heard that Portland now has its two lines to the East, and that they'll be crawling right through Washington. Should've followed our conscience and formed the 'Pacific Republic' like my father—rest his soul—favored. That would have solved a lot of financial and political difficulties—"

"You're right, George Washington, very right. My father saw it the same way—California, Oregon, and Washington.

But there was the war. Are both lines open?" Courtney asked of the railroads.

She listened intently for the answer, not knowing which line would bring Efraim and Lance.

"Open—except for delays and breakdowns. The one leading up the south bank of the Columbia to connect with the Northern Pacific is still in dispute since Villard went bust. The one turning southeast to connect with the Union Pacific's more dependable. The Southern Pacific has taken over the Oregon and California Railroad . . . silver's going through . . ."

Courtney's mind drifted as the doctor talked on—almost stalling for time, it seemed. How was she going to explain to Efraim and Lance? But best not worry about that until she knew the outcome—an outcome she dared not think about.

An outraged cry from upstairs interrupted breakfast and brought the group to their feet. Donolar's face was chalky. Cousin Bella looked carved in stone. Mandy shed great tears without moving a muscle and Mrs. Rueben's face twisted grotesquely. Courtney surveyed the group as if they were from another planet, scarcely aware of her surroundings. She wished she could feel something. Anything. Anything at all. But she seemed to be floating somehere near the beamed ceiling of the sunroom.

Was she all right?

Quite all right (through marble lips).

If she wished to stay here—

Oh, no!

"Then Courtney and I will go alone—"

"Not this time, George Washington. You've kept the family out quite long enough. We all want to be on hand no matter what the outcome." Cousin Bella's voice was determined.

The doctor picked up his bag. "You're right, Arabella. It's a family affair and—"

Without finishing his sentence, Doc George turned toward the stairs. The others followed, single file, like a funeral procession.

"Good morning!" Doc's voice was too cheerful as he entered the room. He opened his satchel, pulled out a magnifying glass, blew on it, and wiped it clean with a white handkerchief. Then he motioned the others to stand back. Nobody need tell them silence was in order. And prayer.

"How do I feel?" Clint moaned. "I am in pain. I am bored. And I'm scared. Does that answer your question?"

"Normal reactions," the doctor said, feeling the bandages to make sure they were wet. Finding them saturated, he commented on what a fine nurse Courtney was.

"Never mind the small talk—or my pulse, which is running wild—just get this devilish mask off my face (his tone softened) so I can *see* my nurse!"

"Patience, my lad, patience," Doc George cautioned.

After untying the thread securing the bandages, he peeled them back layer-by-layer. All the while he kept mumbling, "Ummm-hmmm, ummm-hmmm," which told Courtney nothing. On leaden feet, she inched closer to him.

What she saw caused her to recoil, and for one terrible moment the room swam crazily. She clawed the air for support. *Oh, Lord, don't let me faint—please, PLEASE!*

When the furniture came down off the ceiling and she found her feet still firmly on the floor, Courtney's first thought was that she had less understanding of the eyes than she had thought. She had forgotten Doc George's words, but surely one of them must have meant something different than she thought. When had he told her that Clint's *eyelids* were stitched together? The room swirled around her and again she prayed for control.

"I'm going to remove the sutures now, providing you promise to keep the eyes closed."

Clint grunted and Doc George, with the aid of his magnifying glass, set to work. Then, holding steady hands over Clint's eyes, he said, "Now, in a moment I will take my hands away. Be prepared for darkness, then only vague outlines. We will open the curtains—a crack of light, please, Courtney—that's it. Now, remember, you'll see nothing at first—"

Courtney's heart stopped, fluttered, and then turned over as she waited for the doctor to remove his hands. She heard the voices in whispery prayers behind her. This was her moment of hope. It fluttered in her breast like a small bird fighting its cage for release. But hope, like Clint's vision, was born slowly. She, too, must be prepared.

"All right, keep those eyes closed a second or so after you feel my hands leave your eyes. I'll tell you when to open."

The room was pin-drop quiet now. It was as if all had inhaled simultaneously and were afraid to let out the breath until they knew. Wordlessly they watched Doc George lift his dimpled hand, then at last give the command.

"Open!"

Clint struggled to lift the heavy lids, then closed them again. "I can't see—not an outline—not anything—"

"Give yourself time, Clint. Now open again and leave those eyes open—"

"It's too painful—"

"Do it!"

Clint tried again. Courtney saw it was no use, but if Clint could focus on anything it would be herself. She moved to the foot of the bed. Untrained as she was, she saw the eyes were sightless.

Chapter 14

Life Must Go On

Courtney and the doctor were once more alone with Clint. The others had filed out quietly, their faces as smooth as a pond. But there was sadness in their eyes—the kind Courtney felt in her heart. Sadness and helplessness.

There was utter defeat in Clint's face. Courtney scolded herself again for being overly optimistic, filling him with false hope. Now, even anger had deserted Clint. He simply lay limp while Doc George rebandaged his eyes.

"I'll never see again." Clint's voice was flat with a heart-breaking resignation, meaning that he would no longer fight.

"Of course you'll see again! It's going to take more time—more rest—"

"How long is *more*?"

"Three or four weeks," Doc George hedged, "until we can get the tear ducts back to functioning. As I told you before, the corneas seem undamaged. Tell you what," he said with a feeble attempt at wit as he stitched the bandages on, "maybe you'll develop night vision—like a cat—"

"I'd like to be alone now," Clint said.

"But, darling, I want to be with you," Courtney whispered, reaching for his hand.

"Please, Courtney." Clint pulled his hand away.

The doctor motioned her toward the door.

Downstairs Cousin Bella waited. At the sound of footsteps she rose from the settee, gripping its arm for support. She was visibly shaken. But being Cousin Bella, she would control her emotions.

"I sent Donolar for fresh roses," she said as if it were any other day. "Sit down and we will share Mandy's molasses cookies and fresh-brewed coffee. I suggested that she and Mrs. Rueben deliver the eggs and pound cakes to neighbors in need. Life must go on."

Life must go on. But how? Courtney wondered, nibbling at a cookie when she remembered she had eaten no breakfast.

After pouring coffee, Cousin Bella sat down again. "What went wrong, George Washington? Courtney and I can face the truth. And so will Clint in time."

The doctor spooned sugar generously into his coffee, stirring the substance longer than was necessary. His voice sounded tired when he answered.

"I'd say he hemorrhaged—the blood coming from behind the eyeball where my magnifying glass can't see."

"What can you do about it?" Cousin Bella's question was a near-bark and yet it held a note of faith in her lifelong friend's ability to deal with the flesh.

Doc George gulped down the last of his coffee and set the cup on the marble-topped table beside him. Blotting his mouth with the napkin he had tucked in his vest, he studied a moment, then said he would have to find a specialist. They were hard to find, but he knew doctors who knew other doctors. Just trust him. And trust the Lord. Together they would patch Clint up like new.

"And meantime, as you say, life goes on. Courtney, you have to get out more. Can't have you and your husband in the hospital at the same time—"

"He is not my husband," Courtney heard herself say. "Clint postponed the wedding—"

"I know. I know. But in a few weeks we can arrange to have Big Jimbo here and you two could be married—no, I guess Clint would never settle for that. Too much pride and too much hurt. Well, he's going to have to snap out of it somewhat—help you and Arabella here decide what to do about the mines—"

Courtney jerked erect. "Who's in charge now? The mines *are* operating?"

"Well—yes, but there's mumbling and grumbling. Big Jimbo's there. His very presence preserves order. That failing, he takes the troublemakers on bare-fisted, punching as if he were in the ring again. Says if he can't teach them the love of God, he can knock the devil out of them!"

"The Bellevues? Are they—" Courtney paused.

"I think I'd best take you for a look—and soon."

Chapter 15

Whatever We Must

The next morning, when Courtney took Clint's breakfast tray to him, she heard voices inside the room speaking in low, conspiratorial tones. The door was partially open and she could not help overhearing. Then, overhearing, she could only stand there dismayed.

"—so you see, Donolar, you'll have to play the game with me. Pretend you're my eyes. Understand?"

"I think I do," Donolar said, "but I'll have to talk to the—"

"You're to talk to nobody. That's the game. It's important—very important. Ask no questions. Just trust me."

"Important," Donolar repeated.

"First, you're to find my shoes. Get them from the closet. Then my work clothes. At first you'll have to help me dress. Later maybe I can manage. And I'll need my horse—"

When Courtney heard footsteps, she rushed in—spilling the coffee over Mandy's carefully prepared scrambled eggs and cinnamon rolls.

"Stop!" The force in Courtney's voice sent Donolar cringing into a corner of the dark room. "I'm talking to Clint, Donolar," she said soothingly as she continued toward the bed. "You've done nothing wrong, Donolar—nothing at all. And Clint is right, we'll need a horse. If you will saddle Peaches for me, I'll be much obliged to you. Clint and I will talk alone, if you don't mind."

"But—" Donolar was clearly confused, torn between two people he dearly loved.

"He told me he was blind."

"He is—unless we do as the doctor says. And that includes keeping him flat in bed. Believe me, it's the only way."

"You mean it's sort of like 'Paradise Lost' and 'Paradise Regained'?"

"You might say that, yes," Courtney said of Milton's epic poem. She was busy setting the tray down and seating herself beside Clint.

Satisfied, Donolar left the room, mumbling to himself about the fall of Adam and Eve in the Garden, the rebellion of Satan, and the "New Vision" which was Christ. He never ceased to amaze her, but today she must appeal to Clint. That failing, she would lay down the law!

"Clint—Clint darling—" Courtney reached for his hand, but he jerked it away.

"You just robbed me of my last hope." Clint's voice was one of surrender when she had expected fury.

"Darling, listen to me," Courtney pleaded. "Hope lies in the Lord, and He's going to send us help. Doc George is consulting with people who specialize in cases like yours. But if you damage your eyes further—"

Clint groaned. "Let's face things as they are, Courtney. My eyes are damaged beyond repair. Nobody can restore vision when it's lost. I am blind. Can't you get it through your head? *I'm blind!*"

Courtney burst into tears of desperation. Whatever she had expected, it was not resignation.

At that moment the door burst open and Doc George's cloud of white hair seemed to fill the room. Whatever spaces there were left, his voice filled.

"Let me at this quitter! I'll handle him in quick order. He'll stay put if we have to hog-tie him and bolt the door. Have a heart, Clint. Turn that self-pity into compassion. Can't you see what you're putting her through?"

"I can see *nothing.*"

"How right you are—blind as a bat both ways! Courtney, my dear, Donolar has your mare ready. You go wash up and make ready to accompany me back to the mines. The outing will do you good."

Courtney hesitated, then did as she was told.

Shortly afterward, Cousin Bella having agreed to keep a sharp eye on the patient, Courtney (attired in a wide skirt that made riding easier) followed the doctor's hack into Kennedy Company Headquarters.

The warm sun on her back restored her spirits. The beauty of God's creation was all around her, and she was saddened to think that Clint's eyes were temporarily (*Please, Lord, temporarily*) blinded to the white-capped peaks that probed the dazzling sky. She concentrated for a moment on the gap between the rugged mountains where the train which might bring Efraim and Lance to be with her could pass. Then, suddenly Courtney and Doc George were in front of the Company Store.

Tony was pathetically glad to see them. "Seems like ole times," he said. "Move over, men, you there by the cracker barrel. Cain't ye see a lady's present?"

There was a shuffle of feet on the hobnail-scarred floor as bewhiskered philosophers scurried from the weathered building. In less than a minute, Tony Bronson, Doc George, and Courtney were alone in the maze of cooking pots, washtubs, slabs of bacon, and mining equipment. Courtney inhaled appreciatively. Strange how she had come to enjoy the mingled smell of freshly ground coffee, pickled herring, hooped cheese, dried fruit, and leather. Today her nostrils picked up a new odor, the unmistakable scent of new calico and cologne.

"I had t'add t'my line, else the wimmen would've tarred and feathered me. Come see th' bolts of new fabric—"

Tony led the way to a far corner of the darkened store. But Courtney's nose had picked up a gentle hint of something else—something familiar but out of place here. Doeskin? She followed the subtle, sweet aroma and found them— pair after pair of gloves, some of them bordering on the expensive.

"They demanded gloves too, mind you." Tony's voice was sheepish: "I hope y'll not be takin' offense at their copyin' you. You've lent such a influence on th' wimmen's dress that they're drivin' their men crazy."

Doc George gave a belly laugh. "That's good. It's high time some of those poor, dehydrated lady folks had some color in their lives. But Courtney here, God bless her, has brought more to this valley than style."

"Oh, very true—very true."

Tony inquired of Clint. Courtney moved away, not wanting to hear the hateful words again. She did resolve, however, to resume some of her work here—accompanying Doc George and Brother Jim in their house calls. That is, as soon as Clint's condition allowed her to leave him. Even today she felt ill at ease being away. Supposing he should need her? She would have a quick look around here to determine that all was well, then hurry home to Clint with the good news. Maybe that would lift him from his deep depression.

The doctor seemed to read her mind. "I'll show Courtney around," he told Tony, "then I have to drive on over to the Fort. I want to consult with a couple of young doctors there—not dry behind the ears yet, but they have a stack of medical books a mile high. They also know some specialists—let's go, my dear."

Courtney followed Doc George as he picked his way through coils of rope, lanterns, and rakes that swung dangerously from the rafters. Outside, Ahab waved a sooty hand from his anvil. Courtney waved back at the burly smithy and continued toward the mines.

At the *arrasta* they paused. Obviously, repairs had been made. Fascinated, she watched as tired-eyed, droopy-eared donkeys pulled the pole-shaft round and round the flat rocks and the buckets dropped quartz to be ground into gold. With a little encouragement she could hate this place— the *arrasta* which may have robbed Clint of his vision, the dangerous mines which had emitted lethal gases . . . all of it! But this was Clint's life. She would learn to share in it . . . even love it, if she could. In her mind it was an enormous, shapeless creature with a dozen gaping mouths, not to let out a fortune—as these men believed—but to devour them. With an effort, she walked past the *arrasta*.

At the door of the largest gaping cavern they paused. From far below came the sound of dozens of picks. The noise vibrated and Courtney fancied she saw the frail timbers supporting the rock overhead tremble. There was the creaking sound of iron wheels, and a mule-drawn cart labored up the incline. The two miners were black with soot and dark soil, and the animal blinked in the daylight. Inside it was almost pitch-black, the lanterns swinging back and forth providing the only light.

"Let's go down," she said suddenly, even though her heart pounded with fear.

"Oh, no, Miss—we can't letcha go thar—"

"Right!" Doc George boomed, his voice a command.

Courtney brushed past their protests. The doctor had no recourse but to follow. Together they explored every inch of the mine—Doc George swinging a lantern high enough for her to see the sparkle of minerals in the damp walls. The crew stared at the pair in amazement, stopping work as they approached and removing dirty stocking caps politely.

The doctor shook his round head. "They dream. To them, this mine's spitting out minted coins—big dollar-sized ones."

Courtney nodded, understanding dawning slightly. A dream was a dream, whether it had to do with unearthing a fortune or bringing sight to the blind. She felt a glow just thinking of how she would be able to share with Clint tonight.

Courtney was dirty and wet as she came out of the mine, but she insisted on going into the little church. It occurred to her then that she had not seen Brother Jim. Wasn't he supposed to be in charge here?

Making her way through the dim light which the sun cast through the pines, Courtney walked down the aisle and knelt at the altar. Fervently she prayed for Clint.

"It is not for myself that I ask You to restore his sight, Lord," she implored. "I would marry him if he were blind, mute, maimed—" Courtney's voice faltered, and she cried harder than she had since the accident.

Dimly she was aware of Doc George's voice outside cautioning one of the men to see her home, followed by the sound of his hack as he rode toward the Fort. She should get up and be on her way, but her tears continued to flow, draining from her all desire to move.

It was then that she felt a timid hand on her shoulder. Frightened, she let out a small cry.

"I seem forever to be frightening you. For that I am sorry, but if I can help—"

The voice belonged to one of the Bellevues. She was not sure which—until she looked up, still frightened.

"You're Horace," she murmured foolishly. "I must go—"

"Stay," the voice sounded sincere. "The preacher's going to meet me here. I—I want to become a part of this—"

Courtney found her legs and ran from the church. She did not stop until she reached Peaches. Could she believe this man? Would he follow? She urged the little mare forward.

The sky had paled to a deep rose hue, softly gilding the clouds, as the tired mare carried her up the gentle slope leading to the Mansion. The last rays of the sun struck the uppermost windows welcoming her home. But a million questions roiled in her mind.

Chapter 16

Wedding Gift

Courtney was aglow when she told Clint of her visit to the mines. But she should have been warned by the lack of warmth in his greeting. Yet, refreshed from the luxurious bath that Cousin Bella had earlier prepared for her, Courtney felt that Clint would share her exhilaration . . . would know that she was doing this for *him* because she loved him so much. As a wife, she would be sharing in everything.

"So you toured the mine? I should have known Doc George was up to something."

Clint's words were sharpened by pain. Stung by them, she tried another tactic.

"They are all rooting for you, Clint—even Horace Bellevue. Would you believe he was in the church and told me he was waiting to have counsel with Brother Jim?"

It was the wrong thing to say. Courtney realized that before Clint's sharp retort. How clumsy of her to speak of a man who both frightened and repelled her as if he were an ally!

"I told you I wanted you to have no contact with him or his brother, Courtney."

"But, darling, I thought—I understood that he was working for you—until you get back—or did I misunderstand? I seem to be doing everything wrong these days—"

Clint sensed the tears in her voice and relented, but only a bit. "I keep hurting *you*—we keep hurting each other, unconsciously. We can't go on this way, you know—"

Courtney's backbone went rigid. "What do you mean?"

She was saved from the awful truth of what she suspected by a rap on the door. Cousin Bella announced that the mail had come. There was a letter, a telegram, and a package for Courtney.

Sensing the tension, she said, "So you go down. I brought the business mail up to go over with my nephew."

Courtney brushed away the tears as she stumbled down the stairs. The mail meant nothing at the moment. But only seconds later, it meant everything.

The telegram could mean one of two things: Either Efraim and Lance were not coming or else they were delayed along the way. With all her heart Courtney wanted—*needed*—to see her brother and her childhood sweetheart, and yet some secret part of her hoped that something had forced them to postpone the visit. She needed time with Clint and, yes, time with herself to sort out feelings and make plans after this cruel turn of events.

With fingers that trembled, she tore the end off the ominous-looking yellow envelope. The date told her what she suspected. The message, like their arrival, had been delayed. The two men had taken the Southern Pacific, Efraim said, which was a poor decision—trouble all the way. And now a delay while the rails were repaired in San Francisco, and did Courtney wish to postpone the wedding?

Courtney gave a little mirthless laugh at the question. No, Courtney did not wish it. Clint did! The laugh turned to a dry sob that caught in her throat. How could a love that seemed so right have gone wrong—no matter what happened?

"Oh, Clint," she whispered, letting the telegram flutter to the floor of the sunroom, "it isn't what life does to us—it's what we do to life."

The words were Cousin Bella's, Courtney remembered. Dear Cousin Bella. She had been so patient. Clint's accident, his attitude toward it, and the wall he had built between himself and Courtney must be hurting his aunt very much.

Lance's letter was more outdated than Efraim's telegram. He spoke of his family and of hers. Her mother was still in Europe. Her sister had not been the toast of London on stage but had met some interesting people. He believed she would be marrying a duke something-or-another and that Mrs. Glamora, said not to be in best of health, would remain with her. She too had met another man. But Efraim had told her, Lance was sure.

> *And now, let's talk about you, dear Courtney. Needless to say, I found news of your wedding somewhat of a surprise; albeit, a disappointment. Was I wrong in thinking that we had an understanding, or was I believing only what I wanted to believe? While the Desmond chap must possess all the qualities I lack, should you change your mind, just know that I'm walking behind you and will be on your wedding day. If ever you should turn around . . .*

Courtney's eyes misted over with tears. Lance was still Lance, thinking that the world went on the same day after day . . . while she had grown into another person entirely, a person that her cherished playmate might fail to recognize. Time would tell.

Quickly she read the remainder of Lance's letter. He was coming, as she knew. He was looking forward to seeing the new country—and her. It would be a challenging adventure. Meantime, he was sending Courtney the painting he had done of her old home, Waverly Manor. And something more. From her letters Lance had envisioned the Mansion to be a "rather Gothic" house, he wrote. Intrigued by the pictures she painted on Cousin Bella's blue stationery, he had painted his impressions in oil. It would be an interesting comparison. So he was sending it, too.

How like Lance, Courtney thought, as she stripped the wrappings from the two paintings. He was blest with a wonderful talent and would be a great artist one day, being one of the few who could afford to devote time to his work.

She had expected to feel no emotion at the sight of Waverly Manor and was surprised when a wave of sadness swept over her. Lance had painted in every detail—even the hole in the hedge through which the two of them as children had crawled in order to play together in the great backyards of the adjacent estates. The sadness was born more of what might have been had her mother loved her father, made a home for him, and loved their children as he did. How different an atmosphere she and Clint would create for their offspring—one filled with love that matched their own for each other!

Even as Courtney dreamed briefly, doubt seemed to sprout from the tight band of morning glories climbing the outside trellis like a vindictive serpent. Would things ever be right again? She sighed. Time. In time, all would be well. She must never give up hope.

Determinedly, Courtney withdrew the other painting from its layers of packing. And for a moment she was tempted to laugh as she stared at the fairy-tale castle in a dark wood. It was a regular wilderness of gables and chimneys between countless towers, crumbling gray stone walls mantled in ivy, and mullioned windows reflecting a drift of silver-lined clouds. In that moment she knew that, consciously or unconsciously, Lance had been more inspired by the fairy stories they used to read (back when she was

Rapunzel and he was the Prince Charming climbing to meet her by way of her long tresses) than by her descriptions. Lance, ever the dreamer.

Carefully she rewrapped the precious gift, thinking as she worked of her actual impressions of Mansion-in-the-Wild that night when Clint brought her here. Even then, although she had only met him on the westbound train (under the watchful eye of her governess), Courtney had known she was in love.

She had fallen in love, too, with Cousin Bella and her ancestral "Mansion"—its grounds and grandiose traditions. Courtney had loved the flowering fruit trees that lined up in welcome along the drive, her first glimpse of the lush vegetable garden at the back of the great house, and, beyond it, Donolar's storybook rose garden . . . his Isle of Innisfree.

Hugging the Mansion were the eternal mountains—some cloaked in green, others wearing caps of snow. And everywhere were the meadows, scalloped in flowers.

But her first impression of the great house had been that it did not belong in such a setting—just as Lance's painting seemed to sense. Instead of being the castle he envisioned, the house rambled, bulged, and loomed up in unexpected places. Here and there were strange additions to the early architecture. And, yet, grotesque as it was, Courtney had sensed that the growing Mansion had enlarged to accommodate a growing family, making room for every pilgrim in need. And how right she had been.

Still, she wondered now what Efraim and Lance would think of Mansion-in-the-Wild, its people, and all the peoples of the Columbia River settlement. She had grown to love it here, but it would be new to them . . .

Courtney was so deeply engrossed in thought that she did not hear Cousin Bella come in quietly until she spoke.

"I left Clint to do some serious thinking," she said matter-of-factly. "He seems to have the impression you couldn't handle it should the worst happen, which is nonsense."

"Oh, Cousin Bella, I could handle anything—*anything*—if only he wouldn't shut me out!" The words were torn from Courtney's heart.

"I know, I know, child. Just give him time."

"You—you haven't given up hope too, have you?"

"Of course not!" But the answer came too soon.

Courtney, seized by a sudden despair, flung herself against Arabella Kennedy, her dark head blending into the neat pleats of the bosom of the dark dress.

"Why, *why*, WHY? Why did it have to happen? Why did it have to happen to Clint?"

Cousin Bella stroked her hair gently. "Courage, my dear; exercise that courage I endowed you with. It is you who must help Clint cling to his faith. Let God do the rest."

Chapter 17

Ultimatum

Courtney had walked over to see Cara the day the young doctors came. It had broken her heart when she found the wedding dress, all rents repaired, and the hem finished by hand in almost invisible hand-stitching. The young Mrs. Laughten, although expecting another child, had insisted on finishing the dress as a wedding gift to Courtney, Cousin Bella said. And, of course, courtesy demanded that Courtney pay her a call. And why not take a basket of Mandy's salt-rising bread?

Cara, wearing a sunbonnet that stood out like a cape in back, was trying to bend over her zinnia bed when Courtney arrived with the basket. She apologized for her appearance and begged Courtney to come inside.

"So hot for July," Cara said, wiping perspiration from her small red face with the corner of her apron. "Guess th' summer's gonna be a scorcher. Too hot fer tea, Miss Glam— Courtney, but maybe some juice."

Courtney accepted the berry juice even though she was not thirsty. As Cara prepared it, Courtney looked about the sparsely furnished room, its floors scrubbed bare of splinters and the yellow curtains daintily ruffled. She remembered that the windowpanes, replacing the rough boards, were a gift from Clint. She remembered, too, Cara's telling her what pride her mining husband took in the bright panels of light.

Outside, a few chickens dusted themselves lazily beneath the sunflowers. The family milch cow chewed her cud lazily in a bed of clover just feet away from the house. Three children and another on the way. All those mouths to feed. Life was hard here—hard and impartial. And, yet, Courtney found herself envying Cara Laughten. How could she make Clint understand? Anything she said these days he considered a barrier. Didn't she know, he would ask if she voiced her feelings about the Laughtens, that being penniless was not the same as being sightless? Yet in a way there was a relationship, if Clint would only count his blessings. These people, for instance, could not afford the specialists that Doc George was consulting. Clint could.

It was about the doctors that Cara spoke, breaking into Courtney's thoughts. "We pray ever' night that the doctors with their newfangled ways can bring back the boss man's eyes. Ever' night—we never forget."

"Keep praying, Cara," Courtney managed. Then, with a quick hug of appreciation, she took her leave. It seemed imperative somehow that she get back to the Mansion.

The sight of a fancy rig by the front gate was no surprise. The doctors! Instinctively Courtney knew.

She seemed to reach Clint's room in a single bound. There, hovered over the bed, were—were these men *doctors*? Although neatly suited, one of the shockingly young-looking men had a red, smooth face—reminding her of a freshly plucked chicken. The other, although equally young, wore rimmed spectacles that kept falling down his nose and being impatiently put back in place, while his pale hair stood out in all directions. For a moment she was almost glad Clint was unable to see.

And yet when they spoke, it was with authority.

"Squint your lids together," said the young man who was red of face (a Dr. Ramsey, she was to learn, although the two men addressed each other simply as "Doctor"). "Get the eyes to make tears, Desmond."

"Good, good!" the other said in a voice that sounded as if he were jumping up and down. "Now, Doctor, where's the instrument? I suspect some optic thalamus problem—"

"What kind of problem, Doctor Trevor?" Doc George queried.

"Damage to the masses of nerve tissue in the floor of the diencephalon from which the optic nerves arise."

Doc George scratched his head, obviously perplexed. "This instrument—what does it do?"

"Gives a view of the back of the eyeballs."

"Impossible," Doc George muttered.

But the visiting doctors were not deterred. Courtney lost track of who said what. She only heard snatches of their professional jargon. Dilate the eyes . . . yes, scars on the retinas . . . normal alignment . . . but without surgery . . .

"What kind of surgery?" It was the first time Clint had spoken, and his voice trembled. Courtney was unable to tell whether it was from hope or despair.

"To remove the scar tissue—unless you'd rather be blind?"

"I may be blind anyway?"

"Bear in mind that, although I am not Hippocrates, I have done these operations before. Now, if all will clear the room . . ."

Six hours later the surgery was declared a success—at least, in part. But wasn't partial vision better than none? Now, as to instructions. All was to be as quiet as a tomb (wasn't it already?) . . . no emotional upsets . . . bed to be kept as the doctors had arranged it . . . elevated so the blood could flow to the patient's head. And the rest was up to the patient. Several weeks of bedrest and a good mental attitude. And now, Mr. Desmond must rest. Dr. Lovelace could take over from here. If he needed further assistance, he could reach them in Seattle . . .

And then they were gone, leaving a quiet household. Subdued. Waiting. Praying silently for the future that looked uncertain . . .

Chapter 18

Arrival

Surely there must be something she could do to cheer Clint, Courtney thought wearily each time she left his room. Nothing seemed to pull him from the depths of gloom that he had wrapped about himself like a quilt, the way she used to shut out the world when there was a lightning storm.

The music box hurt his ears, Clint said. And, devout a Christian as he was, he took no comfort from the Scriptures. Courtney read him the story of Job's trials and knew immediately that it was a poor choice. Clint needed comfort and cheer. She read from the Proverbs and the Psalms.

"Do you want me to continue reading, darling?" she would ask. His answer was always "Yes" and nothing more.

When alone, Courtney outlined little themes emphasizing the importance of living one day at a time, beginning with God's creation of the world. "We just have to be patient," she said.

"You should be reading about the virtues of a good woman," Clint said tonelessly.

"Oh, that!" Feeling a flicker of hope, Courtney thumbed her way through the Proverbs and read the passage. "I can't spin fine linen. I'm not even sure that when I open my mouth it is with wisdom," she said lightly, fanning the spark of hope in her breast. "But, oh, Clint, I will rise up early in the morning and serve my household—just give me a chance to prove myself—"

Clint groaned. "You have proven yourself over and over, Courtney. But you deserve better than a blind man."

The hope flickered and went out. "I *have* the best, darling. I love you with all my heart—"

"Love is not enough," he said through stiff lips.

Courtney felt a jolt, as if she had stepped down with all
her might on a step that was missing from a ladder.

" 'Perfect love casteth away fear.' Can't you accept that
you are very probably going to be all right—see again—and
stop fretting? Love *is* enough . . ."

She paused, looking into the bright horizon of being with
Clint again . . . riding the meadows . . . meandering the
happy little brook hand-in-hand . . . pausing on its mossy
brink to share a view of the valley, an apple, a kiss . . .

The vision was so dazzling that her heart felt too large
for her chest. If only Clint could see it—not see, *feel* the
dream with her. But, looking at him, she felt the familiar
sting of shock. His face became guarded, as if the invisible
shutters were drawn against her. His once-open smile was
vague and impersonal.

It was always the same, that transfiguration. Why, then,
did it freeze her heart each time? She should be accustomed
to the change in the man she was pledged to marry. But the
hurt inside her was growing. Could it be that Clint no
longer welcomed her visits? That his love was dying? Or
was it his stubborn, masculine pride? And why did she no
longer feel free to ask him? *Oh, dear Lord, what has happened to us?* her heart cried out.

To escape the gnawing doubts, Courtney consented to ride
across the countryside with Doc George one afternoon. Old
Mrs. Withers was complaining about her liver and Stella
Ferguson, whose twins had the whooping cough, was housebound and would welcome a visit from another woman.

On the way Courtney asked, "Level with me, Doc George.
Will Clint regain his vision?"

"I'm checking his progress daily. His chances are good . . . very good . . . if he'll cooperate. He violates a rule every time I turn my back. And his attitude!" Doc George rolled his blue eyes skyward. "You'd think we'd removed his eyeballs! See what you can do about that."

"I've tried," Courtney said as they drove up to the Ferguson cabin. It was good, she realized, to be around other people. It was also true that when people feel down and out, the best medicine is helping others . . .

* * *

Brother Jim called on Clint unexpectedly. He lumbered up the stairs, each step creaking at the burden of his heavy-weight build. He asked Courtney to make herself ready to call on a few "friends of the Lord" while he spoke to Clint. *Alone.*

Wondering who was looking after the mines, Courtney did as she was told. A few minutes later, dressed in a cool blue pinafore, her black hair drawn severely back and tied with a matching ribbon, she waited in the hall. The door to Clint's bedroom was closed. But the preacher's voice, like his step, jarred the house.

"Don't you go worrying about the mines, my boy. They're being looked after, but the Lord's in need of some trainers in the ring! Now, it's true you've been dazed by a hard blow, but you're not out till the count of ten. The church needs fighting men like you to survive this day of mushy-fisted, jelly-spined, pussy-footin' society. There are enemies within the church as well as without, and it's hard tellin' the sheep from the goats. You're needed, Clint. Now, rise up from that bed when the time is right and hit the trail with me again. You've got to fight, man, *fight*, FIGHT!"

Clint, if he answered, spoke in so low a tone that Courtney was unable to hear. She heard Brother Jim's voice . . . her name . . . and then his voice dropped low in prayer.

The big prizefighter-turned-preacher did not speak of the conversation as she rode with him in his creaking rig across the countryside. He talked instead of new claims that were filed everywhere and the new diggings. Initial assays made no promise of striking it rich, but the small yield of the Kennedy Mines was enough to set men's hearts dreaming.

"The Bellevues? Clint has not spoken of them."

Brother Jim looked at her sideways. "Didn't Clint tell you that Horace had made peace with the Lord?"

"Clint would have no way of knowing. It was I who told him of—of seeing him briefly at the church. He was waiting for you."

"But he's visited with Clint—made arrangements to work for him, sort of on a temporary basis."

"Are you sure that's wise?"

"I don't make the decisions, but I have no real reasons to think otherwise—at the moment—"

Courtney's mind ran in circles. The last phrase made her wonder if the big man classified Horace Bellevue as a true sheep. Or was he possibly a goat? She wondered, too, why Clint had not told her of his half-brother's visit. But, then, she had told him nothing of Efraim's delay. And he had not asked. *It's because*, she thought, *we've stopped communicating.*

Annabelle Bushnell, the spinster who spent her days in bitterness over desertion (so others explained) at the altar by a corset drummer, met Brother Jim and Courtney at the door with her face puckered in a chronic frown. She eyed the pair suspiciously before inviting them in.

"First thang we wimmen hafta larn is bein' cautious," she said in a raucous voice. "Thar's the elements, snakes 'n wolves—'nuff t' make th' blood bile. An' if them fail, there's the weather bilin' yore juices come summer 'n turnin' hit t' ice come winter."

"Come, come, my good woman, it's not that bad. Hasn't the Lord taken care of you so far? You forgot to mention Indians. I see they've spared your pretty hair."

The compliment gained Brother Jim an entrance. Courtney suppressed a smile. The woman's mousy hair was stretched to the top of her head and piled there like a stack of Mandy's sausages.

"Well, git yore readin' done now that yore here," Anna-belle said as Brother Jim opened his dog-eared Bible. But just then Courtney heard the children (which the woman got herself "stuck with" when her sister died of the fever) call out to her down by the brook. Annabelle quickly decided to go down to tell them Bible stories, knowing she had a more willing audience.

"What about the other Bellevues?" Courtney asked as they took leave of Annabelle Bushnell.

"Milt and that Villard woman? They're up to no good, believe me. Homesteaded one of the best places around—and, of course, Alexis has her eye on what she thinks she has claim to—be right glad when your lawyer-brother gets here."

It was then that Courtney saw they had taken the road to the mines. Clint would need a report, the doctor said. Courtney wondered.

It was Horace Bellevue who greeted them. He stepped from the Company Store as if he had been awaiting their arrival. And he looked spic-and-span, far too clean to have been down in the mines. What, Courtney wondered, did he think his job included? She realized then that she did not know. Anyway, she was being too suspicious of the man.

The suspicions lingered, however, as he came to her side of the rig a bit too eagerly and began assisting her without asking. That was another of the characteristics she found distasteful about Horace Bellevue—a bit too eager, as if he were determined to peddle his wares and had a compulsion to do so by making physical contact. He seemed to feel that a casual greeting required a touch on the shoulder or a stroke of the hand. And something in his manner made her recoil.

Today, after she had carefully disengaged herself once she was on the dusty ground, Horace reached out to stroke her hair. "I like it like this," he said. Just a simple little compliment, but the words felt too personal

Courtney hurried toward a group of miners and, to their delight, engaged them in conversation in order to avoid further contact with Clint's half-brother.

Yes, Miz Courtney, th' mines was goin' well.

Their employer—*boss*—would be back soon. No, no news, but the doctors were reassuring. If there should be the slightest hint of trouble, they *would* let Brother Jim know?

Yes, Miz Courtney . . .

The pointless conversation came to an abrupt end when Tony Bronson ran from the door of the store and began yelling excitedly. "Telegraph—uh, telegram—important—says it's to one Miz Courtney Glamora."

Courtney scanned the yellow sheet quickly. "Efraim, my brother, will be here tomorrow. We must get home quickly. Clint will want to know—"

She did not look back to see the shadow that crossed the face of Horace Bellevue.

*   *   *

The giant engine heaved out clouds of cinder-studded smoke which drifted lazily through the sunlit bowers of fir trees hovering over the tracks. On occasion a small puff would plummet downward to where Courtney and Donolar stood watching. Impatiently, Courtney would brush it away.

Donolar was obviously nervous. Courtney tried to reassure him while understanding his shyness and fear of meeting his twin. The "other guest," as he referred to Lance, did not trouble him.

"It will be all right, darling. Just you wait and see," she kept saying. And she meant it.

What *might* not be all right was the meeting between the two men and Clint. He had become more of a recluse than Donolar. While she had never known him to be impolite or inhospitable, Courtney felt a gnawing apprehension at the core of her heart. Clint had almost ignored her when she told of the telegram. When she made mention of the mines, Clint asked for a glass of water, then gulped it down and coughed, spilling the water on the sheet. Courtney wiped it up.

"It's all right, darling."

"It's not all right! And I thought we agreed that you were not to go near the mines—or the Bellevues."

"But Clint," Courtney had objected, "you engaged Horace's services. And I thought you might like a report from me—until you are back to oversee—"

"Don't use that word!" Clint had said shortly. "Courtney, we have to talk—"

"I know." Courtney made her voice gentle but firm. "But not until you're in a better frame of mind, Clint."

And for the first time she had walked out.

All those glowing reports she had written about Clint, she thought as she looked impatiently from face to face in search of Efraim and Lance—they simply were not true anymore. How would she explain? It occurred to her then that she wouldn't have to. They would understand—

And there they were!

Seeing the two of them again, sharing embraces, babbling on about events on both coasts—it was almost as if the two years between had never been. Efraim—dear, dear Efraim, who had handled the affairs of Waverly Manor so efficiently—answered her letters with his usual prompt efficiency, and kept her buoyed up by his promises to come West. And Lance, equally dear, who had made her feel like Her Ladyship even when she was gangling and clumsy. Being such a gentleman, he would have courted her properly and proposed at just the right moment, and they would have been married . . .

Married! What ever could she be thinking of? Certainly she was not handling the situation well. Not well at all.

Turning to look up at her tall, handsome brother, Courtney said breathlessly, "Efraim, meet your brother. Donolar, darling, here is your twin."

Donolar's great, expressionless eyes appeared not to blink and there were white lines of fear around his beautifully curved mouth—so like their mother's.

It was Efraim who made the first move. First a handshake. And then the two were in a bear hug. Courtney felt tears of joy spill down her face and was glad when Lance's fingers laced through hers in understanding.

Minutes later, Efraim introduced his brother to Lance, saying quite simply, "Lance, this is Donolar."

Donolar extended a pale, slender hand. "You will be happy here with Courtney and me—and then there are the butterflies. They're keeping watch while we're away."

Lance Sterling, as genuine as his name, nodded soberly. Events have come full circle, Courtney found herself thinking. I am back at the beginning again . . . meeting Donolar here with Clint . . . or am I further back? Back home with Efraim and Lance?

A lump filled Courtney's throat, suffusing her with tenderness for all the men in her life. Even now she could feel Clint's arms holding her close, his chin resting on top of her head, his arms around her sob-racked body (if he knew how much he had hurt her!). At the same time, she was surprised how time had melted down and she was with her adored brothers—each representing a margin of a different life but linked together by inseparable genes. And Lance! Oh, how she had missed him . . . more than she realized. And, in her lonely, confused state induced by Clint's tragedy and reaction, Lance *was* the Prince Charming he had seemed when he awkwardly kissed her hand in farewell the day they parted at Waverly Manor. There was the same hated black curl falling over his high, intelligent forehead and the same luminous eyes with a mixture of admiration and curiosity, with the maturity that time brings. And she, for a childish second, was his Princess—mature, head held high and carrying herself gracefully, her mysterious black eyes inviting admiration. His!

"I'll check on the baggage," Efraim said, his efficiency bringing Courtney back to earth.

"And I must check on a hotel," Lance mumbled, tearing his gaze from Courtney's.

"Oh, no! Cousin Bella would never hear to that," Courtney protested. And then, as if it needed proving that it was not her idea, she added, "Right, Donolar?"

"Right, Courtney."

Chapter 19

Joy Turns to Sorrow

Dinner was a pleasant affair, far more festive than Courtney would have anticipated. The great house, in its exquisite setting, had been overshadowed by a cloud of melancholy since Clint's accident, but now it seemed to reach out its wooden arms to welcome the guests.

Courtney, who had taken little interest in her dress since Clint was unable to see her, laced herself into a pink calico dirndl and brushed her black hair until it shone with burnished highlights beneath the glow of the copper kerosene lamps. Seated between Efraim and Lance, she felt at peace for the first time in ages. She was uncertain how her brother and friend's presence would help Clint, but somehow it would, her high spirits promised. It just *had* to. Somehow it would be the miracle they were waiting for.

On the way home she had assaulted Efraim and Lance with questions and filled them in on reminders about the big house, its occupants, the settlement, the mines—and Clint's condition.

Introductions had gone better than Courtney expected. Clint was cordial. She was probably the only one who noted the strain in his voice. It had been there all along, but did she only imagine that it was more pronounced when he took the hands the men extended to him?

Arabella Kennedy arranged to have dinner served in the dining room for the first time since the accident. After all, another member of the family had come "home," bringing a guest. She also wore the heavy black taffeta dress that swished with each breath, the one she had worn the first evening Courtney had dined in the Mansion. The dress whispered against the starched whiteness of the linen cloth sweeping to the floor and folding around the pleats of the hostess' skirt.

Again there was the feeling of déjà vu—the same bouquet of perfect roses from Donolar's garden perfuming the room, making her senses reel . . . the flicker of candlelight as Mrs. Rueben extinguished the light from the lamps. Mandy had even prepared a dinner almost identical to the one which had first welcomed Courtney to the Mansion . . . platters of crisply fried trout, mustard greens, freshly baked bread, and a chocolate cake that rivaled Mount Hood in height! There was a subtle air of excitement. And yet—

The significant difference was that the table was set for ten. They were all there—Cousin Bella, Doc George and Brother Jim flanking her sides, Donolar, Courtney, Mandy and Mrs. Rueben, Efraim and Lance—except for Clint. His chair was a grim reminder that the present was different from the past after all. Courtney let the talk flow around her, feeling the glow in her heart extinguished much as the housekeeper had snuffed out the light from the lamps.

"May we have group prayer this evening?" Cousin Bella's question said that it was all settled. "We've much to be thankful for and much that concerns us. Brother Jim, if you'll begin, those of us who feel moved to do so will follow."

Brother Jim's prayer was long and fervent. The others were more brief and to the point. Cousin Bella praised the Lord for Efraim and Lance's safe journey. Donolar asked that his roses keep blooming and that the "evil ones" would not be returning or new ones come to take their place. Courtney's voice trembled a little when she repeated Cousin Bella's praise and then asked God's blessings on Clint, shut away in a world of darkness. Efraim and Lance sat silent.

There was no awkwardness. Doc George waited the exactly appropriate amount of time and then began his petition: "Now, Lord, we've done all we can for Clint, and we ask You to do the rest. Be with us all when those bandages are removed tomorrow—"

Tomorrow! Courtney hoped the Lord would forgive her for hearing no more. She had known the time was near; how she had prayed for time to pass! But now that the critical hour was so near, she felt an icy fear ring her heart. What if—but no! She must not think like that.

She turned her attention to Cousin Bella, who was speaking: "You will find life very different here, Efraim. And it is nice to have the family extended. Too, there are business matters that require a legal mind like yours. I should like to talk to you about that this evening. Tomorrow will be busy . . . and (turning to Lance), Mr. Sterling, we all want you to know that you are welcome at Mansion-in-the-Wild for as long as you care to stay. It is good for Courtney to have you here. Goodness knows the child has been housebound long enough."

Lance favored her with a brilliant smile. "You are very gracious, my dear Miss Kennedy—"

Doc George cleared his throat loudly. "Come, come! Must we be so formal? We're all family here—something you may be unaccustomed to on the other coast, Lance. But, Arabella, you should know better!"

"So I should, George Washington. Suppose you call me Miss Bella and I shall call you Lance."

"Indeed," Lance said gallantly. "Miss Bella it is."

After dinner the doctor went upstairs to check on his patient. Brother Jim followed, saying he wished to have prayer with Clint. Efraim went into the library with Cousin Bella.

"Just us three," Donolar observed, "and that is nice. Maybe you would like to see the Isle of Innisfree in the moonlight, Mr.—uh, Lance. Sometimes the roses whisper at night."

"Thank you, Donolar," Lance said, helping Courtney from her chair. "We shall hope they speak to us—Courtney, do you need a light wrap?"

The roses were magnificent bathed in moonlight, and their headiness was overpowering. Courtney wondered if Lance was caught up in their spell. It was hard to tell . . . he was asking Donolar questions and listening as if the entire world depended on the boy's responses. Donolar, in his delight with so rapt an audience, talked nonstop, his conversation making sense. She was grateful to Lance. But then, one could expect him to be courtly to Cousin Bella and accept Donolar with the dignity he felt all people deserved.

Courtney and Lance walked the short distance back to the Mansion in companionable silence. At the back gate, he paused. In the moon-drenched shadows he looked even taller. For a moment their eyes met—dearly familiar to each other and yet strangers. Lance broke the spell by speaking.

"Are you happy here, Courtney—truly happy?"

"Oh, yes, Lance—very, very happy. I have found love's beautiful dream—"

Lance visibly winced.

"And you will come to love it, too—the countryside, the people, all of it. One feels so close to nature here—so close to God you can almost touch His face when the sky is low, as it is tonight."

Lance looked at the caldron of blue that tilted to spill stars overhead. "Yes, I can see that," he said slowly. "I shall love to paint here—and I shall love being with you again. But," he sighed deeply, "there's something hard for me to explain about Sterling House, where I was born, as was my father, and his father before him . . . can you understand?"

Yes, she could understand. A touch of his fingers, soft as the finest silk, made it easier.

"We must go inside. I feel a slight chill," she said.

"Yes," was all he answered.

*   *   *

Courtney was the only one in the household who was awake when the doctors arrived in the early dawn. Pulling on a light robe, she ran barefoot downstairs to meet Doc George, finding to her surprise that the two young doctors were with him. They nodded to her either in greeting or as if to grant permission for her to be with them as they entered Clint's room.

The red-faced Dr. Ramsey gently lowered Clint's bed. "Let us hope, Doctor," he said to Dr. Trevor, whose pale hair still stood out in all directions, "that time and gravity have done their job."

"And prayer," Courtney whispered. They gave no sign of hearing. Neither did Clint. He had not spoken. The moment was too grave.

"Now, Desmond," Dr. Ramsey said, "We have removed the bandages. I'm going to dilate the eyes, then light a lamp."

Courtney held her breath in the gray darkness. She could see Doc George leaning forward, watching in silence.

"The lamp, Doctor!" Dr. Trevor obliged. "What do you see?"

"Total darkness—as I have for weeks—*nothing*!"

"Time—give yourself time—we have brought special glasses—"

The doctors were leaving! Courtney hurried after them, begging for hope. Maybe, they said. But for now it was the trauma's aftereffects; only time would tell . . .

Chapter 20

End to a Beautiful Beginning

The morning sun had just topped the mountain like an enormous red button when Courtney tiptoed down the hall to check on Clint. She hoped to be alone with him when he made his first steps after the long confinement. The moment belonged to them.

Clint heard her footsteps. "Is that you, Courtney?"

"Yes, darling!" Courtney threw open the door and rushed to Clint's bedside. He was wearing the dark glasses the doctors had left and was already propped up on one elbow.

"Oh, how good to see you in that position! It means progress." Unconsciously Courtney dropped to her knees by Clint's side and buried her face in the quilt covering his body as she reached for both his hands. How she longed to have him hold her, to say something—anything to renew what they once shared. She felt the muscles in his forearms twitch, but he made no effort to caress her.

Instead he spoke. And his voice was so impersonal that she could have been a stranger.

"If you will hand me my robe, I'll try standing—"

Rebuffed, Courtney rose and made her way to Clint's closet. Blinded by tears, she had to feel rather than look for a robe. The brown depths of her eyes were troubled as she took the garment to him. What had menaced the good comradeship they had first known which had ripened into love? Now he was actually her foe—thrusting and retreating. What had she done to destroy that relationship? The germ of fear that had been in her heart all along was sprouting into the conviction that it was more than the blindness which kept them apart. No! So beautiful a beginning could not end this way.

Awkwardly Clint shrugged into the robe. Without speaking, he lifted a hand to Courtney. She tried to lend a supporting shoulder, a gesture that Clint's body language refused. He stood, reeling only slightly, then—taking a white cane— asked her to direct him to the nearest chair.

"Clint, you made it! Oh, darling, you made it!"

"I was never crippled, Courtney."

"I know—" she said uncertainly, then stopped when Clint made a circle of the room with his hand.

"Sit down—we must talk—"

Courtney let herself sink into the chair nearest him, waiting . . . knowing that all was not well . . . that her world was about to be dashed to fragments that might never be pieced together again. But her heart cried out, No, no, NO!

Without turning sightless eyes toward her, Clint murmured, "I am blind, Courtney. Me. Blind." Clint shook his head as if he were unable to comprehend the words he was saying. His pale face looked jaundiced with despair.

"It's going to be all right, darling. You'll see—" Courtney longed to run to Clint, embrace him, reassure him of her love. Not daring, she resorted to the litany that women in love use to heal—reassurance.

Clint drew a long, shuddering breath. As if not hearing her words, Clint went on, "I've known for a long time—and I overheard the two visiting doctors in conversation—"

"Oh, Clint, why didn't you tell me?" Now, precaution tossed to the wind, Courtney was on her knees beside him.

"I—I tried to protect you," he said brokenly.

"Clint," she said, catching one of his hands and drawing it to her face, "touch me—just touch me—"

"Oh, Courtney—you—you're crying." Clint's voice was hoarse with pain.

"I always cry. You know that. I cry when the sun rises and when it sets . . . hearing the church choir . . . Donolar's roses. But most of all I cry when I think something's wrong between us! Clint, I'm pledged to be your wife, your partner, and that means sharing *everything*—the good and the bad—only now there isn't going to be anything bad—*really* bad—as long as we have each other!"

For one euphoric moment Courtney felt rebonded to the man she loved. She believed her words. The difficult times ahead were no threat to her. In fact, they made life all the more challenging. Here was her chance to prove her love, really *prove* it. What better investment could she make of her life than to share it with tiny intimate tokens that would triple Clint's vision—make him see her in a new light, with or without his eyesight?

Courtney was suddenly aware that Clint had withdrawn his hand. "Courtney, listen to me. First, I want to thank you for all you've done. I know I haven't shown my appreciation—"

"I didn't expect that. You've been ill—"

"Just listen to me. I have a request—"

"Anything—anything at all—I'm sorry. You told me to keep still."

"I wish I could tell you how I feel. It's like I've been swimming and somehow got myself caught in the current. I tried to stop myself—or maybe I didn't want to stop—"

Forgetting herself, Courtney sang out, "Love is a perpetual motion. Of course you couldn't stop yourself. We are a part of each other—"

"Courtney, I am trying to tell you something. I want you to release me from our engagement."

Now Courtney was caught in the same current. Her lungs were filling with water. She was unable to breathe. She could barely gasp, "No—just—tell me you don't love—me—"

She waited and waited. When there was no reply, she rose. "I will have Mrs. Rueben get your clothes."

The old insecurities were back. She was rejected . . .

Chapter 21

Questions Without Answers

That night, in her great poster bed—alone and lonely—Courtney lay thinking of her life. What was it worth without Clint? Wonderful Clint, whose love had transformed her from the frightened little girl who felt worthless into a mature woman who knew, if only briefly, that she had everything to give. And where, she wondered bitterly, did that giving get her? Now the man who had performed this miracle had rejected her as had her mother, her sister, and all others in her childhood.

Courtney turned restlessly, plumped up her feather pillow, and tried for a more comfortable position. She wasn't being fair in her generalization. Efraim had always loved her—Efraim and Lance. And they were here now, here to comfort her aching heart. Only in a strangely contradictory way she almost wished they weren't. Was the timing good or poor when Clint—

Clint! The very thought of his name sent her reasoning powers on a million tangents. Questions filled her heart. Questions without answers.

What had happened to their commitments to each other? Did commitments not embrace all circumstances of life? Clint's blindness? Her acceptance of it? Where was love when calamity struck? Was Clint afraid? Where was his trust in the Lord whom he had taught her to trust?

Wearily Courtney turned again, her pain suddenly turning to anger. It must be that Clint no longer loved her. Then he ought to be man enough to say so! He was being stubborn. Mulish. And she should have, for the first time in her life, engaged him in a shouting match! Maybe she could have changed his mind. And then she sighed, the anger—so foreign to her nature—melting away. She could no more change his mind than she could move the mountain range over an inch or enlarge the valley.

The tears came then. Enough, Courtney thought, to send the mighty Columbia River sloshing over its banks. When at last the tears subsided, she lay exhausted, taking a bitter pleasure from the footsteps she heard pacing back and forth in Clint's room while wishing at the same time that they would come down the hall. But the *tap-tap* of his cane told her that there was little hope.

At last she submitted to the fit of exhaustion and drifted into the land of sleep. The only place where dreams are real . . .

Chapter 22

A Time of Transition

August had been a time of transition. Now there was a promissory kiss of autumn in the breeze. Mandy grumbled that the end of the cucumbers, green beans, early tomatoes, and beets had come—but what difference did it make with folks a comin' an' a-goin' as they wuz? There was hope for the fall melons grown from her Georgia seed if Mrs. Rueben would quit chokin' 'em t'death with all that dust she was beatin' from carpets hung over th' clothesline.

The box elders along the creek, stripped of their purple berries for jam, drooped sadly. But the creek itself sang on, although it too sounded a little sad to Courtney's ears.

To the surprise of everyone, including Doc George, Clint learned to move about the house and yard almost as if he had full vision. The doctor was delighted. But Courtney's heart was filled with a new fear. Some inner sense told her that his need was based on getting back to the mines . . . and that there would be no stopping him . . . not by anybody . . . and least of all herself.

She was right.

How ironic life was, Courtney thought sadly, as she watched him, with very little aid from the miners who had come for him, mount his horse and ride away. There was no backward glance . . . well, of course not. But Clint could have waved, if not to her, at least to Cousin Bella, Donolar, Mandy, and Mrs. Rueben, who sadly watched him off.

Yes, how ironic. Blindness, which could have brought

him closer to her, was taking him farther away. Courtney looked past the stream and into the ocean of golden wheat, an ocean which beckoned as the Atlantic beckoned silently to her. Did she belong here now? With a heavy heart, she turned away.

"He still loves you, you know." Courtney jumped at the sound of Cousin Bella's voice.

"He has a peculiar way of showing it," Courtney said bitterly. "Oh, Cousin Bella, what am I going to do?"

"You are going to wait for my nephew to come to his senses. Bright as he is, like George Washington says, he has no more common sense than a horsefly sometimes. Until then, you're to stay here with me, my dear—you, Efraim, and your friend for as long as he wishes. By the way, he's up by the cliff, painting. He thought you'd wish to be alone in your farewells to Clint—nice boy, Lance."

"Yes," Courtney said warmly. "Lance is a love. He— he doesn't know about—about the broken engagement. Neither does Efraim—or anybody else, except you—"

"George Washington knows, Courtney, but depend on him to play mum. And—well, Donolar suspects. The butter-flies, you know—"

For some unaccountable reason the words caused Court-ney to burst into tears. And immediately she was in Cousin Bella's arms.

"There, there, my child, it will work out by and by," the older woman soothed. "Efraim's in town for me and—"

"What am I going to do?" Courtney sobbed.

"Do you want to pray?"

"I wouldn't know what to ask," Courtney said as she wiped her eyes with the lavender-scented handkerchief that Cousin Bella placed in her hand.

"We'll not *ask* anything. We'll just put the matter into God's hands. He'll know what to do."

* * *

Courtney spotted Lance on the bluff where she and Clint had sat sharing the apple, the jerky, and the moment of truth which told them that they were in love. The memory was painful. When Lance waved, she lifted the full skirt with the prairie dust-ruffle and ran.

Gallantly, Lance rose. "I'm glad you've come. I thought you might be in need of a friend."

Tears stung Courtney's eyes. "I will always be in need of a friend," she said. "What are you painting?"

Looking at the canvas, Courtney was unaware of the look which crossed the youthful face. It hinted of the need to say more. "Oh, the landscape—how lovely," she said sincerely.

Heretofore Lance had painted her a flower, a street scene from the New England town where they had spent their childhood, a sunset, and a little fairy-like creature which was a figment of their imagination as children.

But Lance had never attempted a landscape. The beauty of the sweeping fields, the majesty of the mountains, and the strange appeal of the scattered homesteads with their fat chimneys, surrounded by flowers and children, eluded him.

"I want to do portraits, you know." Lance's tone was apologetic. "Will you pose for me, Courtney? Now?"

"I—I'm not sure I am a good subject," Courtney said self-consciously. But she found herself moving toward a rock.

"Here—here on the grass, holding a daisy and just being you. You have a beautiful profile."

Courtney glowed at the praise. The sun was warm on her

back and she felt some of the guilt she had experienced at being unable to help Clint. There was total silence except for the dropping of pine needles and the occasional protest of their presence by a squirrel.

Quite suddenly Lance laid his paintbrush aside. "That's all for today," he said, wiping his hands. "And don't ask to see my work. Somehow I feel this will be my masterpiece."

Remembering the bold splotches of paint that used to stand out on his canvas, Courtney smiled. "Are you a great painter—the way you dreamed of being, Lance?"

"What you mean," he said softly, "is am I happy? No—there remains a lot to do before I reach the destination. But, I am good, I guess. Good, but not great yet. But wait until your face captures the eye of the critics. Then we—"

Lance stopped and bit his lower lip in concentration.

"We must be getting back to the Mansion. Remember my cousin's rule for dinner at six; there are no exceptions," Courtney reminded Lance.

Lance gathered up his materials almost reluctantly. It had been a lovely afternoon, one Courtney had wished could go on forever—like childhood—while at the same time willing it to end. Something inside her pointed a finger of caution lest she wander back too far.

"Did you chance to meet up with any of the natives?" Courtney asked practically, in an effort to crawl back into the body of reality. Their time together was only an antidote to loneliness. It *had* to be.

"Strange that you should ask. But then you always had a way of reading my mind. Yes, I met up with the oddest sort of a chap. Actually, he sort of slipped up on me—a hulk of a man with yoke-shoulders—"

Courtney laughed. "Oh, Lance, you are becoming one of us. You're destined to stay."

Lance's classic mouth crinkled at the corners as she remembered it when they shared childish secrets. But his eyebrows lifted quizzically. "Whatever made you say that?"

" 'Yoke-shouldered' is a native tongue!"

And then the moment was past. "This man—did—were his eyes close together?"

Lance appeared to concentrate, but Courtney felt he knew the answer. Why was he silent?

"Lance?" she prompted.

"Yes—I think so—I wasn't going to mention him. I personally found him offensive."

"Milton Bellevue—"

"Bellevue!" Lance dropped one of his paints and reached to pick it up. "*Your* Bellevues?"

Briefly Courtney told him of the relationship to both her and Clint. "On opposite sides of the family, of course. And Milton is trying to establish claim to a small vein of gold in the Kennedy Silver Mines through some legal rights his wife supposedly holds—"

"So that's what Efraim is working on for Miss Bella! I didn't like the man's looks. And his manner and words were insulting—I'm ready."

Together they walked through the shadows of the forest—the trees so high and thick that only shafts of the fading light sifted in. Their footsteps made no sound on the needle-strewn ground. Then, abruptly, Lance stopped.

"Is it true what Milton Bellevue said—have you broken your engagement, Courtney?"

Courtney's heart seemed to stop, miss a beat, then flutter up to choke her. She strove for an outward calm.

"Don't listen to the man, Lance—please—"

Chapter 23

Chance Meeting

The sun was still behind the fog-wrapped mountains. There were no shadows in which to hide. Courtney, her heart fluttering like the gold leaves of the willows near the creek, backed Peaches behind the trunk of a large sugar pine. Gripping the saddle-fork for support, she leaned forward and peered intently through the mists of early dawn. She was right: Two men stood on the western bank of the stream, and they were pointing at Mansion-in-the-Wild and then in the general direction of the mines. This was Kennedy property. What were they doing here? Even though the day was Sunday, they were trespassing.

Ordinarily perhaps she would have dismissed the scene, deciding that they were only passing through. But caution was her companion these days. Such strange things had been going on. Donolar felt it, and reported mysterious sightings which the two of them decided to keep secret. Now, although she was unable to distinguish the faces, Courtney knew the two men's identity. And when they were joined by a woman wearing a smart riding coat and breeches, but hatless—her flaming red hair a danger signal—Courtney knew she was right. But what were the Bellevues doing here?

Bellevues! So Horace *was* working with Milt in whatever scheme they were contriving!

Courtney's first thought was to confide in Cousin Bella. But she hesitated. Cousin Bella's strength seemed to be ebbing since Clint had left the Mansion and (determined even in his blind state to show his independence) taken up quarters with the men who camped near the mines if their families were not with them. It was Doc George who pointed out to Courtney that Arabella's health was closely aligned with Clint's welfare—most particularly his plans to marry Courtney.

No, Courtney thought now, as she turned the little mare back toward the Mansion before they could be detected. The logical person—in fact, the *only* person—to know that the Bellevues were indeed together was Clint. Having Horace at work in any capacity could be a threat—a threat that Clint would be unable to see. Glancing over her shoulder once more at the rendezvous, she urged Peaches forward, glad that it was Sunday and—

Her thoughts were interrupted by a familiar call, one which resembled a mountain quail. It was Donolar's signal. Courtney reined in at his cabin, where he was picking roses. Dear Donolar—the only person she knew who could make them bloom the year round.

"You saw them too, didn't you, Courtney? I was peering through the cattails—and they came close—I—I'm afraid to be alone. I didn't imagine it—I didn't—"

The great eyes looked at Courtney in despair. Although he was older than she, Donolar was a child—a child she always wanted to comfort and love. "No, Donolar, you did not imagine it. I saw them, and we will tell Clint today at the fish fry. Had you forgotten that Brother Jim plans the community get-together along the river bank after church?"

Donolar appeared to think about the matter. "I—I guess I remembered. I must have because I've gathered the roses—and I saw Brother Jim preparing yesterday's catch. Yes, I will be with you, won't I—'Doing God's will as if it were my own, yet trusting not in mine, but in His alone!' "

Donolar turned again to his roses and Courtney hurried home to change clothes. The fish fry was a good idea. It would serve to reunite the church family, which had been torn apart by epidemics, dangerous gas escaping from the mines, and the threat of the other two Bellevue brothers, who were now out of the picture. The neighborhood women had been baking for days—all sorts of cakes, pies, and probably chicken and dumplings, which some might prefer to fish barbecued over an open fire. Brother Jim was overjoyed at their enthusiasm. They would drive that slippery Satan from the "baptizing banks" of the Columbia . . . send him cringing back to his fiery pits . . . and rejoice!

The air was charged with excitement when the congregation gathered a few hours later. The valley women, most of them in new calicoes or made-over ginghams (and a few wearing gloves from the counters of the Company Store), gathered around the wagons to greet one another and exchange tidbits of gossip while their men tethered the teams. Oh, this was going to be the grandest get-together yet. Brother Jim wore a wide black tie and the ridiculous frock coat he usually reserved for weddings and funerals. He waved and shouted to men who were fording the shallows of the creek and carrying forked sticks for barbecuing the fish. The fire was burning, sending plumes of smoke spiraling through the trees.

Courtney noted that Doc George was hovering somewhat over Cousin Bella, who did look a trifle peaked in spite of her heightened color. She wondered if Clint knew what he had done to his aunt. His infirmity was simply no excuse . . . but how does one make a blind man see? He had chosen to isolate himself, but there was one thing he had been unable to stop, she thought triumphantly: their prayers! Caught up in thought, Courtney failed to see that the worshipers had gone inside. She had stood aside deliberately. Her purpose was twofold: She wanted to avoid embarrassing questions, and she hoped to catch sight of Clint.

As her eyes scanned the area quickly, there was a movement in the sumac beyond the last tunnel of the mines. Clint would not be there . . . an animal . . . but, no! a man and a woman! They were bent over as if looking for something. And then they were gone.

The hymns had begun. Feeling guilty, Courtney slipped in quietly and sat down on the back seat.

"Is it well with thee?" Brother Jim boomed.

"Yes!" Came the answer in unison.

This is a day for rejoicing . . ." the giant preacher shouted in his best ministerial voice.

But Courtney heard no more. Clint had entered without a sound and seated himself just inches away. She hardly dared breathe. *Please, Lord, please,* her heart implored, *let him talk to me today—make things right somehow—*

In a sense her prayers were answered. During the final hymn Clint eased himself from the bench with surprising agility and walked out noiselessly. Courtney followed.

"Clint." The word was a whisper. "Oh, Clint—"

"Courtney!" Surely she did not imagine the note of joy in his voice as color burned his temples. But he did not reach out to touch her. And when he spoke again his voice was concerned but impersonal.

"You really should keep inside, you know."

"I *do* know. That's what I wanted to tell you," Courtney said breathlessly. "Horace is not an innocent bystander, Clint. He's working with Milt and Alexis—they're up to something—"

"That's dangerous talk, Courtney. Now go back to the others. Consider this a chance meeting—" And he was gone.

Chapter 24

A Talk with Efraim

The brilliance went out of the day when Clint left her so abruptly. Somehow she got through the rest of the day, hoping she said the appropriate things, and then—blessedly—the family was on the way home. The woods were shrouded in silence and Courtney could feel everyone's eyes on her. If the others had seen Clint, they bit their tongues to hold back the news.

It was lamp-lighting time when Courtney went wearily to her room. But she sat in the darkness, letting its quietude swallow her up. Through an open window drifted the sighs of the pines and the scent of clover. The little stream kept up its exquisite song—sometimes languorous, sometimes triumphant in its march to the sea. Distantly, the cattle lowed peacefully. But there was no peace in Courtney's heart. She fell into a sort of reverie in which she and Clint were together—love's beautiful dream.

When there was a light rap on her door, Courtney sprang forward, half-expecting it to be Clint. The lamps burned in the downstairs hall, outlining the familiar face of her brother instead.

"Efraim—oh, Efraim!" Courtney threw herself into his arms as she used to do as a child when the world went all wrong. She was laughing and crying at the sight of him. "What kept you? Why did you stay away so long? Oh, Efraim, I'm glad you're here!"

"I must say I never expected such a welcome," he said, pushing her tear-dampened hair from her face. "But,

Courtney, little sweetheart, what is it? It would take more than my absence to upset you like this."

"It's—it's everything. There's so much to say and yet so little I can say to explain matters."

Efraim's arm remained around her as he steered her to a winged chair. "Sit down, darling, and try."

"You, first," she said, wiping her eyes with the handkerchief he supplied. "What did you find out for our cousin? I was worried about you—and about all else here—"

Efraim lighted a lamp and sat down in a chair opposite her. How like Donolar he looked in the pale glow! And how she loved her two brothers. Would the time come when she must choose between them—as if she must choose between coasts?

But Efraim was speaking. "It took time, and it will take more, to dig into the files regarding the rights that Alexis Bellevue insists she owns. I have engaged the help of an attorney who is well-versed in searching out titles, the fine print of original documents, and that kind of thing. So far we have found nothing, but we are dealing with a woman who knows all the angles. Both of us suspect she has something up her sleeve."

"But mustn't it be a matter of record, Efraim?"

"Exactly. But Alexis is crafty and may have documents that her father neglected to have recorded—may even have recorded them herself."

"Then that would give her no claim?"

"That's what we're hoping to establish. Her claim to mineral rights, if it mentions gold specifically—well, we'll just have to see. While waiting, I spent some time at the lawyer's office going through dusty papers and I also made some trips to the mines. Now, little sister, do you confide in me or do I have to play the heavy-handed brother?"

Courtney laughed affectionately. "You couldn't if you tried, but—oh, Efraim, my world has fallen apart—"

"It's Clint, isn't it? Well, let me tell you that he's managing remarkably well. Doc George tells me that the blind develop a sort of seventh sense—"

Courtney's laugh came out more like a sob. "It's too bad they don't develop a sensitivity!"

Efraim covered the distance between them in one stride. Pulling his sister to her feet, he said, "There's something wrong between you two. I feel it. And that shouldn't be. You're very right for each other. Even Lance senses the rightness."

"I think I have failed Lance. I have handled this whole thing badly—just as I always do. I failed Clint, too—"

"Oh, my sweet, sweet Courtney, always bearing the burden of the world on those frail shoulders. Lance came here expecting nothing—at least, you promised nothing. He knew you were betrothed. And, as for Clint, I never knew him before the accident, but—" Efraim reached down to kiss her forehead, "well—I am sure he would make an acceptable brother-in-law."

Would, Efraim? Not will? Courtney wondered just what had made her brother use the conditional. What did he know or suspect?

When Efraim spoke again, it was about herself. "I want you to promise me something, Courtney. Stop this pattern of thinking—of blaming yourself for the mistakes of others. You felt responsible for our mother's unhappiness and it robbed you of a childhood. Hang it all, you are neither responsible for Clint Desmond's accident nor his lack of acceptance. But—" tenderly, "you *are* responsible for allowing it to blight your life. There are others who love you, you know."

Courtney burst into a new flood of tears. "I *do* feel rejected, because I *am*—and I'm worried, too—"

In his protective arms, Courtney told the whole story then. About Clint's breaking the engagement. About Donolar's fears. And about the mysterious behavior of the Bellevues. There was only one matter she skirted . . . her mixed emotions about Lance.

Chapter 25

"Her Majesty"

For several days following, Courtney thought about Efraim's words, wondering if she did indeed carry a needless load of guilt about Clint. It was wrong to turn the situation over to the Lord and yet try to solve it herself. No matter—she found herself unable to resolve the myriad of emotions or dissolve her love for Clint. In fact, she was meeting her mature self for the first time, recognizing that she was the kind of woman who could stand the wear and tear of life and deal with it. There would be a carryover into marriage. She could deal with her husband's moods, but (with a jut of her chin) did that mean she had to humble herself to the point of crawling . . . begging . . . pleading? Maybe it did, she concluded, if the relationship were headed for the trash heap. Anybody could fall in love. It was staying in love that counted . . . and, oh, (miserably again) Clint had not done that . . .

There were other matters she needed to think on too. But thinking time was limited. Both Doc George and Brother Jim were asking her services. Life must go on in the valley. The universe did not center around her and Clint . . . except in her heart.

And then there was Lance. She had been unable to persuade him to attend church or the fish fry. He had to finish the paintings he had begun, he said. And he painted as if he were driven. Most of all, he wanted to complete her portrait. It was to be his masterpiece. They had worked together during almost all the daylight hours. But he wanted to catch a certain feel in the early-morning air. And so it was that Courtney gave him priority of her time that early Saturday.

Efraim had gone to the city to continue his search of evidence or lack of it concerning Alexis' alleged claim. Afterward he planned to stop by the mines. Courtney knew he was doing it for her, and she loved him for it.

The household was quiet as Courtney and Lance slipped out. Dawn was just creeping over the eastern mountains, spraying the dark sky overhead with ribbons of color. It was a fairy-tale world straight from their childhood. And Courtney felt herself caught up in its spell. The mines, their threats, and their foes were raw reality—a reality she sought to escape as she watched the last friendly star twinkle out, listened to the sleepy complaints of the birds, and smiled at the sound of an energetic rooster somewhere in the distance hailing the dawn. Here and there a curl of smoke rose from a cabin chimney.

"Oh, Lance, isn't it lovely?" Courtney tugged at his sleeve. She so wanted him to share the moment with her as Clint had—his beautiful Dream Country which he could no longer see. The thought made her eyes mist over with tears.

And so she did not see the way her companion sucked in his breath as, biting his lower lip and watching her face in the increasing light, he replied.

"Lovely is hardly the word," Lance said. "Beautiful is more like it."

The sun pushed over the mountains through a fleece of clouds just as they arrived at the knoll where Lance enjoyed working. The hills were now painted with a radiance that defied capturing in oil. But Lance was more interested in how the sunbeams danced in her hair.

"Perfect," he murmured and set to work. "Don't move."

Courtney grew stiff from sitting but did not complain. It was important to both of them that the portrait be finished. He worked rapidly, and occasionally they spoke.

"You love it here, don't you?" Lance asked at one point.

"Oh, yes, I love it! Don't you feel its spell?"

"There are moments when I do," Lance said, not meeting her eyes.

"But?"

"I confess a certain disappointment—a feeling that we do not belong here—"

"We? *I* do, Lance."

"There are moments when I doubt that, too."

Courtney jumped to her feet. "Oh, Lance, how could you doubt—after my letters—our talks—and Clint?"

Lance was on his feet, too. And suddenly his arms were around her. "Oh, Courtney, I didn't mean to hurt you, my darling. I love you too much for that. But I understood the wedding was off—"

"I told you not to listen to gossip," Courtney objected, but she did not stir from his arms.

Lance sighed. "I can hope it is *not* gossip. I want to take you home, Courtney—"

"This *is* home." Why, then, wasn't she backing away?

Lance's arms tightened. His voice was hoarse with emotion. "Oh, Courtney, you can't marry a blind man—you—we—"

He felt her stiffen against him and said quietly, "Forgive me—I had no right. If you will sit down just briefly," he said, trying to lighten his voice, "I will show you the most beautiful woman this world has ever seen."

Lance was right. Courtney was unable to believe that she had been the inspiration for the portrait he had entitled "Her Majesty" with his bold initials scrawled beneath.

"Oh, Lance—" Courtney wanted to weep. About the picture. About what could not be. And about what *was*. The treacherous dark-current swamp that she and Clint had sunk into, a condition that none of Doc George's ointments or poultices would cure. Her heart gave an extra pump of love and grief.

"You've a touch of genius, Lance," she whispered. "You are right. You do not belong to us."

Chapter 26

Cara's Cry

Dinner centered around the orange-fleshed salmon that Doc George had caught and Mandy had baked to perfection. He monopolized the conversation about the catch. About the importance of being grateful for the bountiful food here (why, his father had told him of how the men in his wagon train lived on buffalo-liver stew for days!). And about the progress of his patients.

"You're sorely needed, Courtney. When will that picture be finished, young man, so I can borrow your model?"

Courtney wondered if the doctor so much as remembered Lance's name. He never used it, calling him "young man" instead. It was a little embarrassing because it was so obvious that Doc George considered Lance an outsider who was invading the property of another man.

But Lance's manners were faultless as always. "I have completed the portrait, sir. Would you like to see it?"

The question appeared to catch Doc George off-guard . . . just as Lance's next statement caught Courtney.

"I will be taking my leave shortly."

Oh, Lance! her heart cried out. She dared not meet Doc George's eye for fear her expression would reveal something he did not wish to see.

"In which case, of course I want to see what you've done. We all do." He cleared his throat to prompt the others to agree. They obliged.

Lance excused himself and brought the portrait, trying the light here and there before settling on the sideboard holding Cousin Bella's finest china. There the mirror above the cabinet reflected a second Courtney.

There was a gasp of admiration. Words ranged from Mandy's "Now, if that don' look 'zactly like our Miz Courtney" to Donolar's quote from Shelley, "Thou art fair, and few are fairer. . . ."

The talk went on around her, but Courtney heard little except the abrupt request from Lance to be excused from dessert. Courtney laid her napkin, carefully folded like the memories she must fold away, on the table and stood.

"If you will excuse me, too, please," she said in a small voice, "there is something I must attend to—"

Curious eyes followed her from the room.

Courtney found Lance leaning on the garden gate in the velvety darkness. "Must you go?" she asked.

Lance did not turn. "I guess I knew all along it would be like this."

Courtney went to stand beside him but made no effort to reach out. What they had seemed to share was gone. Remaining was what they had always shared . . . a beautiful friendship and a mutual need.

"A part of me wants to go, Lance," she said miserably.

"And a part of me wants to stay."

"It will, Lance. Oh, it will! I will always love you in a very special way."

"But that isn't enough. I hope you will be happy, Courtney—that you will find a way back to this chap who doesn't deserve you—forgive me. I guess you would stay here regardless."

"Yes," Courtney said slowly, the realization coming like a great light shining around her, "yes, I guess I would."

"We'll not say *goodbye*, dear Courtney. I couldn't bear that. Let's make it farewell—and if ever you should need me—"

"I know, darling." Dear, dear Lance. Courtney laid a small hand on his tapering fingers. The hand of an artist, destined to go far in sharing his talent with the world. "You have a rare gift, Lance. I—I just wish you could share it with the Lord—"

The words surprised her more than him. "I find God in nature, Courtney. Does that make you happier about the status of my soul?" There was hurt in his voice.

"Yes and no. It's a start. God is in everything good and beautiful. I learned that from Clint. But I am speaking of a risen Lord—"

"You can pray for me then."

"I always do. Farewell, Lance." She stood on tiptoe and brushed his forehead with a kiss.

"Now, that was a sisterly thing to do." Lance tried for a teasing tone and failed. "We'd better go inside. I must pack. I'll be gone before you are awake tomorrow. It is better that way."

"Yes," Courtney said, then ran through the door and up the stairs to her room where she could weep.

*   *   *

Lance had arranged with Donolar to take him to the train station before dawn. Donolar had agreed, since it would be near evening and "full bright when I travel back alone—the evil ones, you know—"

When Courtney heard the sound of the carriage wheels taking Lance on the first leg of his long journey, she rose and dressed quickly. An early-morning walk around the grounds might serve to clear her head . . . help her face this day. The familiar ache of loneliness was back. At least Lance had given her a choice. It was more than Clint had done. She was close to feeling sorry for herself when a scream split the incomparable dark that precedes the dawn.

It came from the direction of the Laughten cabin. Cara!

Courtney felt her way through the garden, heading toward the frightened woman's screams. When they met, it was near Donolar's "moat," the narrow stream separating the little homestead from the vast ownings of Arabella Kennedy. Lamplight from the cabin windows guided them the rest of the way. Cara was too hysterical to make sense as they ran.

"He jest woke up with a little cough—that's all—and now he's gonna die—die afore my man can git t'see his baby agin'—I could'n wake Donolar. Little John Henry's gonna *die*—"

"Get hold of yourself, Cara," Courtney said authoritatively. "Donolar has gone to take our guest to meet a train and there's nobody who can go for the doctor. You and I must save the baby. Cara, *Cara*, do you hear me? Your baby's life is in our hands!"

Courtney gave Cara a little shake. Startled, Cara stopped screaming. But her eyes were still wild with fear.

"Let me to him!" Courtney pushed past Cara toward the labored breathing which came from a far corner of the darkened room. "And turn up the wick on the lamp."

Cara, still whimpering pitifully, did as she was told. In the flood of light Courtney could see the baby's face—crimson and tinged in blue. He was choking!

She picked him up, as she had seen Doc George do, held him against her shoulder, and patted him gently on the back. He stopped coughing when the sputum came up, but there was a frightening wheeze in his throat and his body was on fire with fever. The rattle in his little chest said croup.

"Do you have any medication in the house? And something we can make a tent from?"

Little John Henry let out a metallic cough, gagged, and began to vomit. Cara began screaming again.

"Cara! Stop it! The baby's life depends on what we do in the next few minutes. Medicine?"

Cara was shaking like an aspen. Her words, through chattering teeth, were disjointed. "Medicine—there's mint and catnip—but my man's gone—"

"Oil of camphor? Some lozenges—you know, something for him to suck on that will help break the congestion?"

"Slippery elm—that's it, slippery elm loz—loz—"

"Never mind pronouncing it. Just get it in a hurry."

Mindlessly Cara clawed at a shelf beside the fireplace. "Here they are—but he's too little—he wouldn't know how to—"

"I know, Cara. I'll have to force one into his mouth and hold it. Now, a sheet for making a steam tent. Water in a small container. We'll burn a candle beneath a pan for steam."

Even as she spoke, Courtney was holding the candy in the baby's mouth. Instinctively he sucked. She breathed a prayer of thanksgiving and then helped Cara drape the crude, hand-carved cradle. Soon the water was giving off steam, and Courtney, lifting a corner of the sheet every five seconds, saw that the little face looked less stricken.

Shortly afterward she said, "We'll have to prop him up a bit, Cara. That will relieve the congestion which might develop into pneumonia. Careful! His rib cage is sore from coughing. He's breathing easier now. So far so good. When Doc George checks on Cousin Bella later today I'll have him take a look—"

Cara panicked. "Don't leave me now. I cain't face losin' him 'n his daddy all at onct—"

"You make some coffee while I watch John Henry. Yes, I will stay, Cara."

The baby suddenly let out a howl of rage, which brought his mother flying from the tiny lean-to kitchen. Courtney laughed. "Relax, Cara. He's coming along fine. He had to have a lungful of air to howl like that. Look, he's sleeping. Now," she said, taking the cracked cup from her friend's trembling hand, "what's this about losing a husband?"

John had left in a huff, she said. Cara wanted him to give up the silly dream of there being gold. He refused. And there were words. Oh, if only she could bite her tongue off!

"Cara, my heart is heavy too. Finish your coffee and let's pray."

"I don't pray good out loud," Cara said shyly.

Courtney set her cup down, checked the baby, and—finding him sleeping comfortably—took Cara's workworn hand in hers. "Just *think* your words, Cara. God hears."

A few minutes later she told Courtney she felt stronger. Courtney took her leave, saying that she must let Cousin Bella know her whereabouts. "When the doctor comes I'll send him over. Maybe he'll take a message to your husband?"

Cara Laughten's face lit up like a full moon. "Oh, if only he will—I cain't thank you enough—"

The two of them embraced. Courtney had a strong feeling as she hurried back to the Mansion that a double healing had taken place: a child . . . and a marriage.

Her heart lifted and soared with an unexplained joy. Yes, she belonged here.

As she crossed the stream her foot caught against a stick and she all but tumbled into the water. At first she thought it was a rock, but then her eyes caught sight of something red. A scrap of cloth, clinging to a stick? She stooped to examine it and saw that the stick was in fact a stake, a recent one driven into the mossy bank. What on earth? Automatically Courtney pulled the stick from the spongy ground and carried it in her hand, pondering the meaning.

Doc George was reining in when Courtney entered the yard. She had forgotten the sharp piece of wood until the doctor's quick eye caught sight of it.

"Hm-m-m, a surveyor's stake. Where did you find this?"

Courtney was forced to tell him. The doctor eyed her sharply. "Know anything about this?"

Courtney admitted that she had some suspicions, then told him about Cara and hurried up to her room to change.

On the way she heard Doc George say to Cousin Bella, "So she heard Cara's cry but not the cry of her own heart . . ."

Chapter 27

Birthday Visit

A week passed. But nobody could say it was uneventful.

Courtney began accompanying Doc George on his house calls again. Together they marveled at the countryside and watched it grow. Everywhere there was change—more cabins, more plowed fields. The countryside was magnificent in autumn.

Courtney half-listened to Doc George's tales about how his family had helped to carve a wilderness into an empire—maybe one of the most prosperous in the Union one of these days. Already was the most bountiful, with its natural resources of standing timber for homes, plentiful water bodies, and fertile soil now waving with golden-headed wheat.

In her mind's eye Courtney saw the valley through Clint's words. "Nowhere else do the mountains serve as pillars to support the sky." *Oh, Clint . . .*

"Still hurting, aren't you?" the doctor asked her one day when he realized she wasn't listening.

"The hurt will never go away, I guess," Courtney admitted sadly, too worn down by her longing for Clint to hide her feelings anymore.

The doctor took the side road leading to the mines then, saying he needed to pick up a few items for Cousin Bella. But Courtney knew the truth: He was giving her a chance to make things right with Clint. And she might if given the opportunity. But Clint was not there. Failing to see him, Courtney asked around. The answer was always the same:

Nobody had seen the boss man. But Miss Courtney shouldn't be worryin' none. He come and went, as she knowed.

No, she didn't know. But on the way back to the Mansion she asked the doctor.

At first Doc George played innocent. "Could be any-where, I guess—"

"You know better!" Courtney scolded gently. "If you know something, tell me. Don't torment me—please."

Doc George's jovial Santa face sobered as he studied hers. "I wasn't supposed to tell," he said, looking a bit like a child caught in the cookie jar who doesn't want to confess his transgression but knows he must tell the truth. "The truth is that Clint has been checking with some specialists—about his eyes, you know. He asked me not to tell you—"

"I'm surprised that he would mention me at all," Court-ney said dryly. "The prognosis?"

"Both good and bad. There's no reason why he can't see. But getting him to understand—or for doctors to find a cure—is another matter. It's psychosomatic."

"Meaning?" Courtney leaned forward to watch the doc-tor's lips. She must not miss a word.

"The relationship between the mind and the body. Clint's eyes are perfect now. The blindness before was a physical thing, but being trauma-induced . . ." Doc George spread his dimpled hands in question. "Who knows?"

The news should make her heart a little lighter. There was hope. And yet it was a hope she did not feel.

*　　*　　*

Saturday was Cousin Bella's birthday. Mandy baked a black-bottom chocolate cake that looked too big for the washpot. Courtney, watching her prepare the batter, asked if she would make a small cake for Cara. When it was iced, Courtney took it to the Laughten cabin. Cara was overcome with the gesture, praising Courtney for being a "midnight angel" and bringing out a rosy baby for her to inspect.

"How many child'urn will you and Mr. Clint be wantin'?" she asked. Then, looking remorseful, said, "I shudda kept quiet."

"It's all right, Cara. I think a dozen would do it!"

Together they laughed, then Courtney started home, carrying a small gift that Cara wanted Miss Arabella to have.

Something prompted Courtney to stop where she had stumbled upon the surveyor's stake. It had not been replaced, and Courtney was about to move on when there was a sudden parting of the buttonwillows and a man emerged. It was no surprise to her that it was Milton Bellevue. What *did* surprise her was his boldness at trespassing so near the Mansion. And his words!

"So *you* are a spy too?"

"What are you doing here—and what do you mean?"

"What I am doing here is none of your business. And what I mean is that if you open that pretty little mouth of yours, I'll tell what I witnessed. Do we understand one another?"

"No," was all that Courtney could manage. She must get past this man. If he had the nerve to come here, he would stoop to anything. But his bulky body blocked the way.

"Let me spell it out. I saw that tender little love scene up there on the bluff between you and that city slicker and I won't hesitate to tell my beloved half-brother. Brothers should share things, don't you agree?"

"Let me pass!" Panic was rising to Courtney's throat.

"Not until I'm sure you'll keep still."

Courtney clutched at any straw. "If Clint knows you're here—"

"I wouldn't be worrying about that. What would you say if I told you he has Horace spying on you?"

"I wouldn't believe a word of it—go away—"

At that moment there was a soft whistle like that of a quail. Donolar! She ran forward, and when she turned to look Milton Bellevue had slunk into the shadows.

*　*　*

Courtney took Cara's gift to Cousin Bella, who looked strangely excited. But of course! It was her birthday.

The excitement continued as Cousin Bella opened the handmade sampler and held it up for Courtney to inspect. Her eyes were shining with a light that Courtney thought had gone out to stay. Did Cousin Bella know some secret?

Now she was holding up the sampler for Courtney to inspect. Courtney frowned in concentration but was unable to make any sense of the yellow mesh in which Cara had punched yarn to make some sort of strange design.

"What is it?" Courtney asked. "Cara is so clever with a needle, but this eludes me."

"Study it carefully," Cousin Bella said, holding up the little rectangle to catch the fading light of the afternoon.

Courtney twisted her head and tried to refocus her eyes. She was about to give up when suddenly there it was! It was so clear that she wondered how she had missed it. The meaningless brown yarn was not the design. Instead, it lay in the yellow spaces between: JESUS.

"Sometimes," Cousin Bella said slowly, "and, believe me, Courtney, it has taken me until recently to realize this— sometimes we think we have to stand on a mountaintop to see His face. Actually, it looms up in the valleys between—just when we need it most!"

"Oh, Cousin Bella, what a beautiful thought!"

For some unaccountable reason tears spilled down her cheeks. Life was making more sense to her.

She longed to ponder the thought. But Cousin Bella was saying in her gruffly affectionate way, "Now, stop the tears, my dear. You don't want to spoil an old lady's birthday! Besides, we're having a guest for dinner. You'll want to look your prettiest."

Courtney came downstairs promptly at six o'clock. The grandfather clock announced her arrival. The others were gathered at the table and being seated. A chair was pulled out for her and she sat down. It occurred to her that the family was unduly quiet. And then she saw why.

Clint's chair was not vacant!

The rest of the evening was a blur in her memory. There were candles and roses. There was talk and laughter. There were best wishes, singing, and prayer. But Courtney only remembered Clint's dearly familiar face. And something else! It had been he who seated her.

The meal finished, there was more talk. And then suddenly Clint was holding her arm and, as if he had 20-20 vision, was escorting her up the stairs. Did she talk? That too was blotted from her memory. Courtney only knew that she never wanted the moment to end.

"I wish I were back to stay," Clint said at the top of the stairs.

"Oh, Clint, I do too," she whispered as if in a dream.

Then abruptly he said good night, and, with the aid of his cane, made his way down the hall to his room. She must call him back. She must. She *must*. But the moment was past. Clint's door closed behind him.

Sick with disappointment, Courtney threw herself onto her bed, still fully clothed, and cried until she was exhausted. Did she doze? She must have, for she had the sudden feeling that she was not alone. She lay very still, her eyes half-closed and her heart pumping as if it would burst. The full moon outlined a man at her door. His hand was on the knob—tentatively.

Courtney remembered then that she had neglected to close it. Was Clint here to close it to insure her privacy? Or was he wondering if he should come in? There could be no doubt as to his identity, and such a great yearning encased her that she longed to call out an invitation.

Instead, she pulled the bedclothes around her neck and feigned sleep. Whatever move Clint made must be on his own.

And then the shadow disappeared as suddenly as it had made an appearance. Down the hall she heard Clint's door close quietly.

Surely tomorrow . . . but tomorrow came and Clint was gone.

The family refrained from saying much about Clint's birthday call. And Courtney's sleep was filled with the same beautiful dream . . . Clint beside her . . . and they were encircled in a rainbow that bathed both mountains and valleys between with scarves of color . . .

Chapter 28

Moment of Decision

When Efraim came home he was filled with news. News, he said, which would affect everyone in the household. But first he must talk with Courtney.

It was a blue-ribbon day. Monday, to be exact. And to be more exact, it was the Monday which dismissed September and welcomed October with the smile of autumn. The Mansion and surrounding forests were drenched in sunshine. Mandy had the washpot boiling outside for the "whites" which could still be line-dried. Mrs. Rueben was doing what she had done in the spring, beating rugs on the clothesline until Mandy had finished the "bilin' " and started scrubbing on the rub-board. Cousin Bella was going through some papers brought home by Efraim, and Donolar was picking rosehips from the bushes which had finished with their summer bloom.

"Nobody would miss us if we stole away and sat on the bank of the stream—up where Lance did his painting," Efraim said. "It seems like a good day for a picnic."

Courtney knew by the sound of Efraim's voice that he wished this part of the talking to be kept private. She was curious and somewhat apprehensive as she helped Mandy prepare a small picnic hamper with blueberry muffins, hard-boiled eggs, and thick slices of ham.

There was little breeze as they trudged up the slope, so the dew, like squares of gossamer, lay in patches along the trail. The trees were silent as if waiting. At the top, where the stream twisted into a triumphant waterfall, Efraim spread a blanket on the grass. Courtney dropped down on it, drawing her knees up to her chin with her arms, and sat—as she had when she was a child—curled in an egg-shape.

Efraim stretched out full-length beside her. "I have grown to understand and admire your young man," he said.

"Clint? I guess he isn't mine anymore." She fought at the sob that caught in her throat.

"A lot of that depends on what you want in life, Court-ney—which is what I brought you here to talk about."

"You're holding something back—"

"Lots of things. But, first, I want you to know that I'm sorry that Lance left. I know how you must feel."

"Nobody knows—quite." She stifled a sob then, letting go of her knees and covering her face with her hands.

Efraim pushed himself upright and pulled her head to his chest. "Cry it out, little sister," he encouraged tenderly, and then looked frightened at the tempest of sobs that shook his sister's slender body. "Was saying goodbye that hard?"

"It's—it's just everything. Oh, Efraim, you'll think I'm a crybaby—and I'm not! I've become a part of this place and it has become a part of me. But I have *feelings*—"

"We all do," Efraim said softly. "Do you feel like talking now?"

Courtney drew back and dabbed at her eyes. She tried a smile with a camaraderie she did not feel. "Yes."

"I want you to know that I've reached no decision, but I have a wonderful opportunity to enter a law firm back home—a once-in-a-lifetime kind of thing. Two of the men who have been helping me search out this Bellevue thing are weary of the hard life and—"

"You're going, aren't you?" Her heart had hardened to stone.

"I told you I had reached no decision. And if I do, darling, you are welcome to come along. In fact—"

Courtney shook her head sadly. "No."

"No? Are you sure, Courtney?"

"Very sure, Efraim. This is where I belong. But," and her voice broke, "I didn't want to lose you and Lance—"

"It's not settled yet, sweetie. And until it is, it can remain our secret. I'm not sure," he said, looking up at the towering mountains, "that I can leave you and Donolar. Even Cousin Bella has grown on me. I will not urge you to come along in case I go. I guess you really do love Desmond!"

When Courtney nodded miserably, Efraim said, "Then see him through this. Strange that I should say that." Efraim's voice became pensive. "Yes, very strange when my profession demands just the opposite—that of seeing *through* others."

"Our background made us suspicious of others' motives, I guess," Courtney said slowly, the idea being very new to her. "I learned so young to be wary—would you believe that I was convinced Mother and Cousin Bella had made some sort of arrangement to have Clint marry me?" Then, pausing uncertainly, she said in a small voice, "Oh, Efraim, you don't think it's possible—"

The question was interrupted by Efraim's gripping her arm in warning. With his free arm he pointed to the brow of the hill. And there, standing as if captured in one of Lance's paintings, stood one . . . two . . . three . . . a *pack* of hungry-looking animals. They were no more than a stone's throw away. Their tongues hanging out, their eyes wild, they stood outlined against the noonday sky.

"Timber wolves," Courtney whispered in terror at the sinister scene. "Probably after sheep in the meadows below—but—they've been known to attack *people* if hungry enough—"

At that precise moment there was the distinct whistle of a mountain quail. Donolar! Donolar coming to check on them. Donolar having to pass so close to the wolves he could touch them.

Without thought of her own safety, Courtney sprang forward, calling her brother's name. Efraim ran after her in an effort to stop her. "Courtney! The farmers will see them!"

Suddenly a barrage of shots rang out, the echoes sounding like an army shooting its way through the gulch as sound ricocheted from mountain to mountain. The wolves slunk into the timber. If the creatures saw their possible human prey, they gave no sign.

But Donolar was terrified. He ran to Courtney whimpering for protection. Her comforting arms were about him and Efraim's encircled them both. They belonged together. They were family. Surely God would make Efraim see!

Shaken, it was hard for any of them to do justice to the lunch. Donolar tossed the leftover muffins to the trout swimming like rainbows in the clear stream while Courtney and Efraim repacked the hamper. They were still quiet as they hurried down the slope.

* * *

During dinner Cousin Bella and Doc George bombarded Efraim with questions, stopping only once, and that was to listen to Donolar's account of their encounter with the wolves.

"How many times have I told you to be careful, Courtney?" Doc George boomed. "There is more than the human enemy here. There is danger and more danger—which makes life interesting, but challenging. Clint had his reasons for not wanting you to be out alone—"

When he paused to take a drink of water from his goblet, Cousin Bella asked Efraim if he cared to share his finding with the family.

"Of course," he obliged, "although there remains much to be investigated. The Bellevues have no grounds, as I am told they once claimed. On what grounds is a question, other than their relationship to Clint, which was foolish, as the relationship is on their mother's side. Alexis, of course," he frowned, "is another matter. She let go of the few shares but does hold an unrecorded document giving her back the right to gold, but only on those shares."

"That would be minute," Cousin Bella said. "There must be more to her troublemaking than that."

"It's complicated," Efraim admitted. "It seems that at one time, a couple of generations ago, her father and this railroad fellow, Villard, had some kind of company called the Worthington-Villard Alliance. They had a right-of-way through this valley which spanned the river—"

Courtney told him about the surveyor's marker she had stumbled onto. "Are they surveying in an effort to find the original lines—and do they cross Cousin Bella's property?"

"It's possible—well, probable that they've engaged the services of a surveyor. But it is highly unlikely that he would turn up anything significant."

"If they found something you call *significant*, what is the purpose? No engineer in his right mind would attempt a railroad through here," Doc George said.

"This is just a wild guess. But *if* the right-of-way easement is still in effect and *if* Alexis can establish her claim to any gold in the area and *if* there *is* gold . . . I think you can see it's an exercise in futility . . ."

Efraim's voice faded away, but in the glow of the candles worry lines were clearly visible in his tired face. Courtney recognized the look.

"What is it, Efraim? Are we in some kind of danger?"

"Yes—yes, there is that possibility. Failing, as you can see they are sure to, the two of them are not above retaliating—"

"Two of them, Efraim? What about Horace?" Courtney persisted.

"Off with his head!" Donolar muttered.

Efraim seemed not to hear his brother. "Horace seems to check out all right. In fact, he has been a big help to Clint—"

"Spying on me?" The words were out before Courtney could stop them. And, at the astonished look on the faces of all who sat at the table, she felt compelled to relate Milt's words.

"There seem to be no secrets in this group," Efraim smiled. "A rather nice way to be, you know. In a sense, Milt was right. Clint has him watching out for you to protect you in case there is any kind of caper from the other Bellevues. But as to spying—well, that's a good enough term, I guess. But it applies to Horace's watching every move that Milt and Alexis make. Naturally, this is not to go beyond these walls."

Mandy rose from the table and returned wearing a smile like an acre of sunflowers. In her dark hands were cinnamon-scented apple dumplings.

There was coffee in the library. Courtney did not join in the conversation. Her eyes were fixed on Cara's gift and its joyful message. Jesus in the valleys, Cousin Bella had said. What a blessed thought! A thought she must cling to no matter what the future brought.

Good nights were said, and Efraim said he would accompany Courtney upstairs. On the way out of the library, she paused beside the sampler.

"Can you read this, Efraim?"

"Jesus," he said to her surprise. Then, looking a little sheepish, he admitted that Cousin Bella had helped.

"I'm glad, darling," Courtney said. "We'll both work on you."

"It's easier to see His sunshine in this part of the world," he said softly, "and especially in the new you."

She squeezed his hand, daring to say no more. Was she comfortable financially now that she had the small legacy their father had left for her and Donolar? Quite, Courtney assured him. There was a small amount deposited to her account in the East, Efraim said, money he had found in another fund when Mother's "royal husband" used up the rest.

It had been an eventful day. But Courtney thought neither about the Bellevues nor the trust fund when she retired. She thought about Clint, wondering why he would have others look out for her and not do so himself.

Chapter 29

Ghosts of the Past

There was superficial calm in the Mansion. And the feeling reached throughout the valley. Courtney could sense it when she accompanied Doc George as he made his rounds. She could feel it at the mines, when Brother Jim told her that Clint had entered a hospital for further testing. Where? The towering giant, who declared himself in charge while Clint was away, was vague. Could be Portland . . . Seattle maybe . . . but all was well. Well on the surface, Courtney felt, but so was water. The depths were where danger lurked.

Doc George said he knew nothing of Clint's decision. His look of displeasure told her that he disapproved. No use. No use at all. His place . . . well, never mind . . . best he, George Washington Lovelace, learn to recognize his *own*! He cleverly steered the conversation to Efraim. So good to have him. A very thorough lawyer. He hoped Efraim would find himself a nice wife and stay put in this land of opportunity.

Underneath the calm—routine, really—a storm was brewing. Smiles wavered. And tremors of the hands of those closest to her betrayed their disquiet to Courtney. It was an air of waiting. Courtney waited too, not knowing for what.

Never did she dream what a dramatic role Cousin Bella was to play. The beginning of the end started with her.

The mid-October dawn was creeping through an open window the morning she heard Mandy's familiar voice singing, " . . . when dey ring dose golden bells fo' you 'n me . . ."

She stopped in midmeasure to knock softly on the door to Courtney's bedroom. "Y'all awake, Miz Courtney?"

Courtney smiled affectionately. The motherly black woman would never drop the formality of a title before her name, no matter how many times she was reminded.

"Come in, Mandy—oh, my goodness! What is this?"

"Miz Arabella, she dun ordered breakfast up here."

Mandy was arranging the tray on a marble-topped table beside the bed before Courtney could recover from her surprise. Cousin Bella had not done this since she came up to share breakfast with her the first day after her arrival. There was no time for questions. Cousin Bella was there, her dignified presence filling the room.

"You may go, Mandy. And thank you," Cousin Bella said in dismissal.

When they were alone, she said, "I thought it was wise if we went back to the beginning. Here, butter yourself a sourdough biscuit, and there's honey . . ."

Yes, honey, ham, and steaming-hot coffee. An exact replica of two-and-a-half years before. What was the occasion?

Cousin Bella set her violet-sprigged cup down, a signal that the meal was over. "Remember how we prayed *after* the meal that first morning?"

How well Courtney recalled her own effort, a little recitation from childhood. It was dear Cousin Bella who taught her the difference between talking *about* God and *to* Him. When she nodded, the older woman bowed her head.

"Heavenly Father, guide me in what I am about to say. Put the words in my mouth which will guide the two young people I love to follow their hearts—not making the same mistake I made, letting my foolish pride stand in the way . . ."

Courtney did not hear the rest of the prayer. She was puzzling over the meaning of Cousin Bella's words.

"You may open your eyes now," Arabella Kennedy said matter-of-factly. "I have something to show you."

Without further ado she reached into a pocket of her wide black skirt and pulled out a small box. She lifted the lid to reveal what looked like millions of opulent seed pearls. Courtney recognized them immediately as the adornment taken from the quaint cap she was to have worn had she and Clint been married as planned. She had never known to whom the cap belonged. But she was about to find out!

"Mine," Cousin Bella said simply. "Mine to have worn had pride not stood in the way—"

"I don't understand—*yours*?"

Arabella Kennedy sighed. "Ah, yes, my dear, why is it that the young can never fathom that those over 50 have loved? Or, if they think of us at all, assume that all remaining is the friendly glow of remembrance—stars that once streaked across the sky and have burned out? That we remember only the bright light and are no longer warmed by it!"

Cousin Bella's voice was bitter, her manner hostile. But Courtney knew that the emotions were directed at herself, that she had been hurt early in life. And now the ghosts of the lost love came back to haunt her as she saw—or thought she saw—the same pattern in the lives of her and Clint.

Courtney did not speak, but she realized that Cousin Bella was right as usual. It was true: She herself had given no serious thought to older people's hurts. Any talk she had heard directed to a later-in-life relationship was the subject for jest. Or, as her cousin said, just memories of fires burnt low. How wrong she had been!

Cousin Bella had regained her composure. Her melancholy had gone. She was directing her attention to Courtney.

"Do you really want to let go of Clint?"

"Of course not!" Courtney cried out without reserve.

"Then why did you?"

Courtney's stomach knotted in remembrance. "I didn't—I mean, it was he who wanted out—"

"But you let him go."

For a moment their glances held. Then the levity was gone.

"You let him go when he needed you so desperately."

"Clint doesn't need anybody—least of all me!"

Bitterness welled up from the very pit of her soul. How could Cousin Bella, who claimed to have loved, misunderstand?

Abruptly Cousin Bella was herself again—kind and unobtrusive—as she reached and caught Courtney's hand. Seeing that it was ice-cold, Cousin Bella's tone changed.

"Oh, my dear, don't think of me as a meddlesome spinster who knows nothing of love. Think of me as a woman who has loved and lost. Some things just never change—the give-and-take between people who love each other enough to get themselves engaged in the first place. Surely you both were very close then—planning on the forever-after kind of relationship that bids children welcome. And, if I'm right, it's worth fighting for no matter which of you walked out on the bargain."

"We both did, I guess," Courtney said slowly. "Oh, Cousin Bella, don't cry about us—we—I—I don't know how to repair things. Don't cry—you're breaking my heart—"

"I'm crying for us both," Arabella Kennedy said. "And when I can stop this silly display of emotions—wouldn't you think I would know better at my age?—I want to tell you a story of the foolish virgin."

Dear Cousin Bella. Courtney leaned over and laid her cheek against the silver-streaked head until she stopped crying.

"Once upon a time there was a young woman who was all business like her father before her. Marriage, like machinery, had to function in a certain fashion, with no variance. Into this hardheaded young lady's life stepped a handsome, dashing young man who was struggling to complete an education and support an ailing mother. I can still see her, hear her—that woman I allowed to ruin my life."

Cousin Bella paused. "But nobody can ruin a life, Courtney. Nobody except ourselves. Not even a whining, self-centered woman who is first a reluctant mother and then a clinging vine who cannot part with her only son—"

"But didn't he, her son, see this?"

"Yes, he saw—and asked me to wait. I waited while my dress hung limp in the closet. I waited until he finished school. I waited until the woman was gone. And then I grew tired of waiting—tired of being tossed aside, *used*. And, with wounded pride, I let go just when he was trying to build a practice—"

"He broke your engagement?"

"He offered. And, foolishly, I accepted—thinking, always thinking he would be back. And then," her voice trembled, "eventually he found somebody else—"

"What happened then, Cousin Bella, tell me—"

"She was a restless social butterfly. There was never a real marriage—no understanding, no forbearance, no children. And when she died, he came back to me. Ah, but mind you, I was having no part of playing second fiddle—so I let him go again. Don't let it happen, dear Courtney—don't suffer as George Washington and I have done!"

Chapter 30

Entry in the Journal

That night, alone in her room, Courtney sat by an open window contemplating the strange story that Cousin Bella had shared with her. The news was shocking, but why? Yes, why hadn't she guessed long ago that there was more between her cousin and the doctor than strong friendship? Once they had loved as she and Clint had loved. Why, Courtney wondered, did Cousin Bella, whose accumulated knowledge now translated into wisdom, still hesitate? It was plain to see that the old ache remained. Actually, the situation had been nobody's fault. More circumstances. Why, then—

Sighing, she let the darkness wrap around her, feeling a reluctance to light a lamp. One-by-one the stars twinkled on. How many of them would shoot across the sky to burn out before she made another effort to see Clint and beg if she must to be a part of his life—make him understand that now was the time to recapture what they had lost . . . before it, too, was but a tender memory?

Somewhere in the distance there was a rumble of thunder, portending the possible first storm of the season. The air had grown damp. Courtney closed the shutters on the front window and was about to pull down the sash when she caught sight of a night rider. Even in the gathering dark she recognized her brother. Her heart fluctuating between tension and hope (both unexplainable), she hurried down the stairs, hoping that their cousin had retired.

She was wrong. "Is that you, Courtney?" Cousin Bella called from the sunroom. She, too, sat in the darkness.

"I didn't intend to disturb you, but Efraim is here and I'm afraid something's wrong—"

"Wait! I will light a lamp." The room was flooded with light, showing Cousin Bellla's face to be drawn and gray with the fatigue of thinking. "I want to apologize, my dear, for doing the very thing I promised not to do—interfering. I was never able to withhold my adamant opinions—and that's why I lost out on love—"

Courtney ran to her and embraced her warmly. "Maybe it isn't too late, Cousin Bella—for either of us! And don't apologize. I'm glad we talked—oh, I must let Efraim in—"

Minutes later the three of them were sharing coffee and Efraim was talking endlessly. Clint had returned, he said. Courtney's heart gave a double-beat of joy at the news, but she forced herself to wait for more that was sure to follow.

It did. The Bellevues had absolutely no right to *anything*, but they were bent on stirring up trouble. There was gold, lots of it, they told the silver miners. They must not believe Clint Desmond. They must stand up for their right no matter what it took!

Cousin Bella's face was ashen. "*Is* there more gold?"

"No, the small vein has played out."

"Does Clint know there's trouble?"

"Yes, but not the nature of it—"

"Oh, Efraim," Courtney cried out, "what *is* the nature of it? Is Clint in danger?"

"We all are, darling," Efraim said. And for the first time she saw how white his face appeared in the lamplight.

Cousin Bella set her cup down with a clatter. She had regained her composure. If there was a crisis, it must be dealt with.

"What do the miners propose to do, Efraim?"

Efraim inhaled deeply. "It could mean simply laying down their shovels and picks. Some of the wives want them to return to farming—give up the dream of striking it rich. I hope it's that simple. We could talk them back on the job, for they have to earn cash for food even while clearing the land and waiting for crops to mature—"

One part of Courtney marveled at her brother's understanding of the needs of families in the valley. The other part thought of the immediate threat. "Or what else might they do?" She asked.

Efraim spread his hands and examined them closely. At last he spoke. "Stirred up, there is little telling. There could be violence. Now, look, it's not all bad news. At least we are forewarned by Horace. Milt is still in the dark about his brother's playing double agent for Clint—as far as we know. And there's Brother Jim. He believes in stamping out sin—"

"But not sinners!" Cousin Bella said.

Managing a chuckle, Efraim said, "They wouldn't risk it! Now, what I want you to do is be on guard—first, for your safety and Donolar's, then for anything suspicious. I will be in touch."

Efraim reached for his sweater. He wasn't going away again surely. He must not. He knew nothing of this country and its ways. "Efraim—please—" Courtney grabbed at his sleeve.

"You know Clint and the others need me. I will be checking on you. And Courtney." Efraim shook a playful finger in his sister's face. "Don't try anything foolish!"

Courtney tried for a smile. It was wobbly, but it was enough of a smile to fool her brother.

Efraim hugged them both. Then, as quickly as he had come, he was gone. Courtney's heart was heavy, but Cousin Bella glowed with a certain pride. "Efraim's adjusting," was all she said.

Again Courtney was upstairs. Her room, although large and boasting high beamed ceilings, felt too small to contain her thoughts. She threw open the sash and opened the shutters. The night lay close and soft. There were no stars now, and the only breeze seemed to be that which played among the branches of the sheltering fir trees. They stirred and sighed to foretell the coming storm . . . and something more. "We have been here for generations—like this house and all who enter," they whispered to the scented breeze.

Courtney wondered. Then, as lightning lanced the sky, she drew away from the window and, without lighting a lamp, undressed and lay across the bed thinking. *This house has a past which even the trees share in. But a future? It has never known the joyous laughter of children—huggable, mischievous boys and innocent-faced little girls with their fingers crossed behind them when they pretend to have no fear of the night's monsters.* And, unless Courtney herself slayed the monster of pride, perhaps the Mansion would never know . . .

During the long night the thunder growled and the very elements seemed to quake with fear. Courtney buried her face in the down pillow and told herself over and over that the house had weathered many storms . . . that it, like the trees, had sunk roots deep here . . . that she would survive, just as she would survive the storm which separated her from Clint.

Chill air whipped in at the window, making sails of the heavy drapes. Courtney rose then, secured the window, and took out her journal for the first time since Clint left. "Dear God," she wrote: "Preserve me until tomorrow and I will go to him . . ."

Chapter 31

Secret Journey

The frail girl on the little mare made her way quietly out of the stable. Peaches found the road by instinct—or did she hear Courtney's prayer?

There was total darkness even though the Laughtens' rooster was predicting the dawn. The rain had stopped, but the sky seemed to swing low as the forest closed in around them. Time and time again Courtney saw the gleaming eyes of animals and just as often told herself that they were not predatory. Peaches had made the trip to the mines before. "We'll make it, won't we, girl?" Courtney whispered, wondering whether she was addressing the mare or its rider.

There was no sound except for the little stream which rippled along beside her. And then the silence was broken by the sound of branches sweeping aside to let someone or something pass, followed by the soft thud of feet on the carpet of needles. Pale light sifted through the treetops now, just enough to reflect on a pair of gleaming eyes as some creature of the forest bent to drink from the busy stream.

Scarcely breathing, Courtney drew Peaches to a stop. The eyes disappeared momentarily as a branch swept between her and the animal. Squinting in the pale light, she waited until the eyes reappeared. Then, momentarily, she relaxed. The enormous eyes belonged to an antlered buck. Undoubtedly, he was testing the grounds for safety before signaling his mate to follow. And then she froze with horror.

A bloodcurdling scream filled the forest as a lithe shape sprang out of nowhere like a silver flash. Courtney had never seen a mountain lion, but instinct told her what this evil creature with slaughter-filled citrine eyes, with wide-open mouth with teeth like yellow daggers, was, and what it was about to do. Did mountain lions, like wolves, move in packs? Should she retreat? Or would that alert this animal or its pack? All this she wondered in a flash. Then she realized that she had no choice at all.

Some primitive urge for survival had stirred inside Peaches. With a wild neigh she reared on her hind legs, almost throwing Courtney to the ground, and then she sprang wildly into the uncharted forest. Courtney was not sure of the direction. She only knew that she too felt the urge for survival. She pleaded in vain with the little mare to stop, but nothing was going to slacken her speed.

Courtney too had panicked. The last she remembered, they were speeding without direction through overhanging brush. Brambles caught at her blouse and tore into her flesh, and then Peaches stumbed and she was pitched forward on her face . . .

Something warm touched her cheeks. Courtney lay death-still, conscious only of breathing in and out and of the heavy beat of her heart. She must be alive. But why was she numb? Why was all sensation gone from her body, which seemed devoid of bones? And why was there a throbbing ache in her head as if she had slept on a stone for a pillow?

Again, the warmth on her face. The sun? Where was she and what was she doing here?

And then memory came with a flood of horror. The deer! The poor helpless deer must have perished, and, in sacrificing his life, saved hers. But for what? Now the animal stood ready to devour her. What mattered the spasms of pain in her legs? Any moment could be her last . . .

But why the waiting? Why didn't the creature consume her? Or did mountain lions, like coyotes, go through some bloody orgy?

A soft whinny restored her senses. "Peaches, you've come back," Courtney whispered in awe, daring to open her eyes for the first time. "But how are we going to make it?"

Warily, Courtney felt for broken bones. There were none, but every inch of her body must be scratched and bruised, and her clothes were in tatters, exposing her body to the rising sun. She must find help. But how could she mount the little mare? Which direction would they travel? And how could she face anybody with her flesh exposed like this?

Praying for strength, she tried her legs. They worked. And Peaches was patient with her many tries to get astride.

Courtney let Peaches follow her nose. This part of the forest was unfamiliar, but didn't animals have instincts that human beings lacked? The trees seemed to grow closer together, as if in conspiracy not to let them pass. Here and there were grassy areas, appearing like scatter rugs embroidered with the residue of earlier-blooming Indian paintbrush, shooting stars, and camas lilies. So beautiful and yet so lonely. Mare and girl may have been the first to traverse the grounds—except for Indians.

The clearing came suddenly. One minute they were among the conspiring white and Douglas Fir and the next they were in broad, open daylight. And voices! She heard voices! She must call out for help. What kept her from it Courtney would never know. Perhaps it was Peaches' sudden stop, as if her delicate nostrils picked up the scent of danger.

At first Courtney was unable to tell which direction the voices, low but angry, came from. Her eyes scanned the steep canyon wall to the right. Nothing—or did something move in the grove of trees beyond? Quickly she looked to the left in hopes of an exit. And then, to her utter amazement, she saw that the mines, the Kennedy Company places of business, and the Church-in-the-Wildwood lay below.

But between her and safety was a great gulf made up by the steep, chalky cliff and the wide stream at its base. Yet something told her that only there would she find safety.

Before she could consider any possible plan for descent, the voices grew louder. Out from the crevices in the cliff to the right of her stole two sinister shadows. At first Courtney thought they had seen her even though she stood statue-still behind a great rock.

"The miners—are they ready?" Courtney would know that raspy, satanic voice anywhere. It belonged to Milt Bellevue.

"They're ready." The voice, quieter and more steady, was that of his brother.

So Horace *was* a part of his schemes, Courtney thought at first. And then she realized that they were arguing.

"Don't do it, Milt—you've taken it too far—"

"You've seen nothing yet! With the miners laying down their picks, we'll close the Kennedy outfit for good—no matter what kind of info that uptown lawyer dug out—saying Alexis was entitled to nothing—"

"But there *is* nothing, Milt—I saw the papers. What's more, he's got a restraining order to prohibit any of you and your men from the area. Maybe even called in the militia—"

"What are you, a turncoat?" Milt hissed at his brother. "Ah, so that's it! You fell for the Glamora gal—took advantage of the boss man's blindness. I heard it rumored—well, it's too late now. The men have orders to torch the church, then the rest of the buildings. All it takes is my signal—"

In the same instant Milton Bellevue pulled a shiny blue object from his leather belt. A gun! And any minute there would be the final signal. It mustn't happen. Not even if it cost her life.

Courtney screamed with a volume that rivaled that of the attacking mountain lion and took a strange sort of pride in the thousand echoes she heard in the valley below . . . even as she felt the ground of the narrow ledge on which she stood give way beneath her. And suddenly she was whirling . . . whirling over jagged rocks, cruel nettles, and low-hanging vines that clawed at her but refused to break the fall.

There was a sudden cold that froze her limbs. And for one more conscious second Courtney knew that she had sunk into the watery grave below . . .

* * *

What Courtney did not see or hear as she fell was the end of the scenario, the parting once-and-for-all of the Bellevue brothers.

Milt, crazed by the knowledge that Horace had betrayed him, turned in sudden fury, aiming the gun at his brother. "I might as well make the shot count, you traitor!"

His downfall was brandishing the gun over his head. The split second was enough for Horace to grab the arm holding the weapon. A kick on the shin did the rest. Caught off-guard, Milt dropped the gun. Then he fell into a pitiful heap and began pleading for his life.

"Clint will want to know what a wonderful gunman you are!" Horace jeered, picking up the weapon. "There they are—marching just like you said they would, but not in your direction. They're fishing the girl from the water!"

Chapter 32

The Darkness Is Past

It was like a circus, Courtney thought hazily. A circus with the usual three rings. The tent was a blue-vault of sky, the backdrop was steep cliffs, and the supporting poles were the towering trees that seemed to shoot up like green rockets. One of the side rings featured a motley crew of clumsy gunmen marching off to jail. The other was filled with excited people, all of them talking at once.

A poor Gretel she'd make (Cousin Bella's voice) . . . leaving crumbs scattered every which where . . . the note in her journal telling her destination . . . Peaches gone when Donolar went out with her oats . . . and then those tracks on the muddy trail. But praise de Lawd, we dun found you-all (Mandy). The scrambled-together English and German would be Mrs. Rueben . . . and what was Cara doing here? The crowd swirled . . . Efraim, saying he was staying if there was going to be a wedding . . . Brother Jim's voice above them all . . . let the doctor through . . . he would take care of the hooligans first—"Stench in the nostrils of the Almighty, they were"—and then there would be a prayer meeting . . .

The lights on the sideshows faded. And the sound effects began. First, the triumphant song of the creek as it emptied into the rapids of the river. Then the comforting sound of a steady *pick-pick* saying that it was business as usual in the mines.

There were no spectators then for the main show—the ring in which Courtney and Clint were undergoing a miracle . . . one far greater than those who had discreetly left the arena could have envisioned.

The sun, like a spotlight, burst from behind another cloud bank and shone on Clint's wonderful face. Slowly, then with a burst of clarity, Courtney saw the tall, lean, litheness of him . . . the skin made copper by sun and wind . . . the formidable strength of the jawline. And the eyes . . . oh, the beauty of the clear, blue depths she knew was there even behind the dark glasses.

"My darling, my darling—my *darling* . . ." Clint groaned.

His arms went beneath the wetness of the mummy-wrap of the heavy blanket in which somebody had encased her. He held her tightly, covetously, and she knew that he would never again let her go.

"I love you . . . I love you . . . I *love* you . . ." Clint was raining kisses mixed with tears on her cheeks.

Oh, dear God, how I love him! Courtney's heart cried out. But when she spoke it was to say ridiculously, "Oh, Clint, I am a mess—"

And then the miracle! "You are not—you look beautiful—"

"Clint!" "Courtney!" They screamed one another's names simultaneously. And then they were both talking at once the way they had done before. The way God intended. The way it would always be.

"You can see—*really see*? Oh, my darling!" "I see a pair of enormous brown eyes in an innocent, Madonna face—as I have seen it in my dreams—" "And behind them are banked fires that have never gone out, Clint—I've kept the dream alive—oh, praise God!"

"You mean—" Clint drew back humbly. "You mean—that you'll have me back after all I've done to you? Oh,

Courtney, I've suffered—my stubborn pride made me think I was less than half a man. You should have thrown me out!"

"No, no! I should have held on. But my old fears of being unwanted—cast aside—"

"*Unwanted!* Oh, Courtney—Courtney," his voice was hoarse with unshed tears, "you are still wearing the ring."

"Of course! It means that I am going to marry you!"

"Enough already!" Doc George, who may have witnessed it all, pretended to be just arriving on the scene. "Let me have a look-see at this brave little creature who calls herself afraid. And then, a quick look at you—"

"I can *see!*" Clint's announcement sounded as if he did not believe it himself.

"Of course you can see," the doctor said as if it happened every day in the week. "Your vision was returning all the time. But, trauma-induced, it took trauma to make *you* see!"

"I can't believe it." After the examination the doctor shook his cloud of white hair in disbelief. "You seem to be none the worse for all you've been through. I'm going to swab these cuts and scratches—and the bruises will go away in time."

"Like those in her heart, if God will be merciful to me," Clint said in a low, broken voice.

"God is always merciful," Doc George said as if he had a more direct line. Then he took out the great pocket watch that was so thick it bulged from his vest and laid it on his knee. In that squatting position he took both their wrists firmly and began counting as if to synchronize the heartbeats.

"Well," he said at length, "you two cannot go back, you know. You'll never be quite the same. You'll be stronger!"

Courtney knew that it was true. Even as the sun grew weaker and the air took on the shimmering quality of another shower, she knew. And that would be the starting of a rainbow.

From the church came familiar strains:

> Amazing grace! How sweet the sound
> That saved a wretch like me!
> I once was lost, but now am found,
> Was blind, but now I see.

The valley had heard of the miracle. Courtney snuggled against Clint's hard chest as he tenderly placed her inside the doctor's hack in preparation for going home. "This time," he said huskily, "I refuse to wait for your birthday."

Courtney nodded happily. "And I want the seed pearls put back in my wedding cap."

Clint did not understand. But Cousin Bella, who had come to join them, winked slyly at Courtney.

"Donolar!" Arabella Kennedy called in a loud, clear voice that gave no indication of her recent fragility. "You take our rig home. Efraim may occupy my seat. I'll be riding up front with George Washington!"

The ancient buggy lurched forward, tossing Courtney closer to Clint. His grip tightened as he whispered, ". . . the darkness is past and the true light now shineth!"

Courtney forced her arms from their wrappings and wound them about the neck of her future husband. Fear and regret were twin thieves that had almost robbed them of a life together. Now the Lord had banished the robbers as He had once banished the serpent from the garden.

The rain had gone and day was fading. Above Mansion-in-the-Wild a bold harvest moon played hide-and-seek with fleecy clouds, remnants of the storm which had passed. Stars appeared timidly, then shone with polished brilliance.

The great, white light of faith-renewed shone round about Clint and Courtney. All else was but a dark preface to love's beautiful dream.

Dear Reader:

We would appreciate hearing from you regarding the June Masters Bacher Pioneer Romance Series. It will enable us to continue to give you the best in inspirational romance fiction.

Mail to: Pioneer Romance Editors
Harvest House Publishers, 1075 Arrowsmith
Eugene, OR 97402

1. What most influenced you to purchase **LOVE'S BEAUTIFUL DREAM**?
   - ☐ The Christian story
   - ☐ Cover
   - ☐ Backcover copy
   - ☐ _____
   - ☐ Recommendations
   - ☐ Other June Masters Bacher Pioneer Romances you've read

1. Where did you purchase **LOVE'S BEAUTIFUL DREAM**?
   - ☐ Christian bookstore
   - ☐ General bookstore
   - ☐ Other
   - ☐ Grocery store
   - ☐ Department store

3. Your overall rating of this book:
   ☐ Excellent   ☐ Very good   ☐ Good   ☐ Fair   ☐ Poor

4. How many Bacher Pioneer Romances have you read altogether?
   (Choose one)   ☐ 1   ☐ 2   ☐ 3   ☐ Over 3

5. How likely would you be to purchase other Bacher Pioneer Romances?
   - ☐ Very likely
   - ☐ Somewhat likely
   - ☐ Not very likely
   - ☐ Not at all

6. Please check the box next to your age group.
   - ☐ Under 18
   - ☐ 18-24
   - ☐ 25-34
   - ☐ 35-39
   - ☐ 40-54
   - ☐ Over 55

Name _____

Address _____

City _____ State _____ Zip _____